NORTH OF THE BORDER

NORTH OF THE BORDER

Judith Van Gieson

University of New Mexico Press

Albuquerque

WITH THANKS TO IRENE MARCUSE

FOR HER ADVICE AND ENCOURAGEMENT

© 1988 by Judith Van Gieson
Published by arrangement with the author
University of New Mexico Press paperback
edition 2002

Originally published by Walker Publishing
Company, Inc. 1988

Library of Congress Cataloging-in-Publication Data
Van Gieson, Judith.
North of the border / Judith Van Gieson.—
1st University of New Mexico paperback ed.
        p. cm.
ISBN 0-8263-2886-5 (alk. paper)
        1. Hamel, Neil (Fictitious character)—Fiction.
        2. Albuquerque (N.M.)—Fiction.
        3. Women lawyers—Fiction.
        I. Title.
PS3572.A42224 N6 2002
813'.54—dc21   2001055528

For the missing and the dead

NORTH OF
THE BORDER

1

"EVERY LIFE IS sacred, even the tiniest life. Jesus was a fetus too."

Easy to tell where that was heading. The clock radio had switched stations on me in the course of the night, and I'd ended up with KFLQ, Family Life Radio. It happens sometimes. I reached over, punched it off, and found the Kid sleeping on the next pillow. He wasn't at his best this morning: pale as a statue, black curls plastered to his forehead, skinny and jittery as an aspen. He was only twenty-four years old, but already he had fine lines beside his mouth and worry lines on his forehead. He was working too hard, a mechanic in the shop by day, an accordion player at El Lobo Bar at night, and sending all the money "back there," I supposed. I couldn't remember when I had seen him last, but when he appeared at my doorway earlier that morning, a street dog who had fetched me an accordion, what could I say? I let him in.

"You awake, bitch?" I whispered, tapping him gently on the shoulder.

"Chiquita, please," he replied, pulling the pillow over his head.

I let him sleep; he needed it. Getting out of bed, I climbed over the accordion, went into the bathroom, and took a shower. It was a day, like most days, to dress as a lawyer. They say that nothing should detract from the competence of the presentation or the brilliance of the mind. If a client notices your clothes, they are the wrong ones. Not noticing what I wore but remembering you are what you eat, I had a slice of cold pizza and a cup of Red Zinger with honey.

I blew a kiss at the Kid and let myself out. Home is a luxury apartment complex called La Vista; luxury means I have gold shag carpeting, a swimming pool, and a sauna that works sometimes. The vista is rolling rock, jagged cactus, and gray hulks of mountains—a mile of elephants, Georgia O'Keeffe called them. I noticed it was a clear day, the sky was still blue, the mountains were in place, and the Kid's truck was parked in a No Parking zone. Truman, the night watchman, had probably gotten too drunk to notice, or he would have been pounding on my door, too.

My car is a Rabbit—El Conejo, the Kid calls it—with "brecas" that squeal and a hole where the tape deck used to be. It took a walk one night when Truman was down in the laundry room rinsing his throat. The state is New Mexico, the town is Albuquerque, a flat place in the midst of mountains. The prestigious law firms are downtown in vertical buildings with blank faces and banks on the ground floor. I'm out on Lead in a one-story place that not too long ago was somebody's house. We've got pebbles for a front yard and a thistle that blooms with poisonous purple vigor in the summer. Me and my partner, Brink: Neil Hamel and Brinkley Harrison, Attorneys at Law. I negotiated the streets of Albuquerque—Silver, Gold, Copper, Coal—and ended up on Lead, wondering if this once I might see Brink's car or even Anna's—Anna is our secretary—in the driveway ahead of me. Not this time.

My office keys were in my purse. I keep them on a ring that has a long plastic handle with NELLIE embossed on it in gold letters. It was down there somewhere among the Kleenex, the packs of Marlboros, the glasses, the notes to myself, and a tube of Ortho-Gynol cream and a derby in a traveling case that I used to carry in case of emergency—a remnant of better days. Now when there's an emergency, it's the Kid, my place, the middle of the night. The key ring was

2

big enough; I should have been able to find it. It was a gift from a former lover who got tired of seeing me fumble my way into buildings. It was a conceit of his that my name is Nellie just because he called me that, but it's not; it's Neil. I was named after my father's brother, Colonel Neil Hamel, of the Tenth Mountain Division, who was killed by an Alpine avalanche near Cortina, Italy, on a cold December night in 1945. I kept telling the guy, *"Neil—my name is Neil,"* but he didn't listen. I've got a key ring to prove it.

I found the keys eventually and let myself inside. What was once a perfectly ordinary one-story frame and stucco home was now an equally ordinary office. The living room is our reception area, the two bedrooms are Brink's office and mine. The kitchen, where we keep the Mr. Coffee and the Celestial Seasonings, is in the rear. It's a cozy place, but it needed cleaning. There were dust balls under Anna's desk, and the *New Mexico Magazine*s on the coffee table were two years old. I made a note—*Tell Anna: get the place clean*—and put it in my purse. I didn't plan to stay this morning, just to pick up some papers on my way to Santa Fe to talk to an assistant DA about a DWI. That's what we specialize in: DWIs, divorces, bankruptcy. If it comes our way, we take it.

I have a big wooden desk with carved panels that once belonged to my father's other brother, Kerny, an attorney in Ithaca, New York. The desk overflowed with papers. It might be a mess to some, but it was a precise mess; I knew where everything was. I took the file off a pile on the southwest corner of the desk and put it in my briefcase. Then I watered the spider plant and picked some dead leaves off the grape ivy. The window behind the ivy was open a few inches, I noticed, and I wondered when I had forgotten to close it. I'm not good about windows and doors; whatever I've owned worth stealing is already gone. The graphite tennis rackets, the microwave—the Cuisinart, even—all belong to my ex-husband, Charles. I haven't replaced him, or the appliances either. I make toast in the oven, and when it comes to tennis, I watch it in black and white on my nine-inch TV. Some guy in a white shirt and a Mormon haircut came by the office the other day, selling religion, I thought, but the product turned out to be word processors.

"State of the art," he said, "user friendly."

I laughed. Anna makes do with a twenty-year-old Olympia. She may be the user, but what she uses is never friendly.

"If we got a word processor, what would she have to complain about?" I asked Brink.

"Us," he replied.

The Rabbit gagged when I started it again. I made a mental note to call the Kid and take the car to the shop to see if it needed a tune-up. I can hit all the green lights on Coal if I maintain a steady pace—a creeping thirty—but some dipshit screwed up the sequence, a low-riding blue Chevy. He squeezed in front of me on Ninth, slowed down at Eighth, cut me off at Sixth, and made my brakes squeal like a wounded pig. The Rabbit coughed, stalled, gagged before I got it started again. *"Pendejo!"* I yelled, and sat on the horn.

He leaned out his window and grinned. "Hey, sweetheart, how's it goin'?"

That's the way it is around here: you tell them they're an asshole, they think it's a pass.

I turned down Second, across Lomas, got on the interstate, and headed north sixty miles to Santa Fe, the state capital. The highway, some people say, is the best if not the only place to think. It has to do with the motion, the space, the inspiration of the top forty. If that's true, I-25 is a thinking person's paradise. Once you get out of Albuquerque, there's little traffic. The mountains recede into the purple beyond, and there's nothing between you and them but space and an occasional tumbleweed. The sky is vast and blue and empty. In a place as empty as this, sometimes the only diversion is yourself; sometimes that's not enough. It can be a relief to see a storm breaking over the Jemez in the west, the rain dropping like a gray sheet and lightning skittering behind the clouds. I wondered what thoughts had passed through the heads of all the drivers who had driven this road and what had been the outcome. The Waste Isolation Pilot Project, a planned depository for nuclear waste commonly known as WIPP? The A-bomb? Los Alamos, Santa Fe, it's the same highway.

After the Santo Domingo Pueblo I-25 was under construction. Day-Glo orange barrels warned me of what was ahead. Earthmovers roamed up and down beside the highway, bellowing and raising clouds of brown dust. I choked and rolled up the windows. A man in a hard yellow hat stepped into the road and waved traffic to a halt. He was a mechanical toy, and I was at the mercy of his ticking arm. Go. Stop. Go. He let me pass, and I leapt up the pink cliffs of La Bajada gaining a lead on the earthmovers when the Rabbit coughed once, choked, and died on me. It happened so quickly, I hardly had time to get off the road. Semis with chrome stacks and Keep On Truckin' flaps whizzed past, shaking the Rabbit on its rubber foundations. I tried to re-start the engine. There was a long silence, a whir, silence; the car was dead.

I had an inkling of what was wrong: a clogged fuel filter caused by sloppy maintenance and cheap gas. Cheap gas: you pump it yourself; it saves you money, it costs you money. What was my client, Joe Feliz, going to do without me? He had been caught doing sixty in a zone where the limit was thirty, and he was probably guilty as hell. I could imagine him in his own defense: "I only had two beers, sir, honest." Who would ever believe Joe Feliz?

A Dos Equis semi passed a truck that was passing me. It was too much horsepower in too close proximity and no place for Neil Hamel. I got out of the car, climbed a grass-less knoll, and considered my options: I could hitch; I could not; I could let the sun make a raisin out of me while I waited for someone to stop and offer a helping hand. In their pleasure at stripping the skin from an already naked

5

landscape, the earthmovers grunted loudly. A red Mazda pickup truck with a white racing stripe came up the hill, hesitated, then came to a stop at the island in the middle of the road. The driver leaned out the window, cupped his hand to his mouth, and went through the motions of yelling. "Can't hear you," I yelled back. He gestured at the futility of speech, and I climbed down the knoll. The smell of diesel was thick on the road, a husky seductive smell that reminded me of Mexico, of the buses and the promise of a beach at the end of the road. Mexico—it took me both forward and back.

"Hi," the guy said as I reached the truck and leaned against the passenger window. "How you been?"

"Peachy."

"What's wrong with your car?"

"Stalled. Can't get it started again."

"Not getting any gas?"

"Right."

"Might be vapor lock."

"Might, but I don't think so. I think it's the fuel filter."

"If you wait a while, it could clear itself, but I'll take you to Santa Fe if you want to call somebody."

"You think it could clear itself?"

"Could."

"I'll give it a few minutes and see what happens."

"Okay, I'll wait with you. Come on in and get out of the sun." He opened the door and motioned me into the cab. I climbed up and sat down beside him. He offered me a cigarette, which I accepted, and some water from a mason jar on the floor. He had jagged teeth, which gave him a sinister dimension, but otherwise he wasn't bad-looking. Skin, tan; hair, brown; body, slight but muscular; height, medium; age, late thirties, an age that had gone through a lot of changes to arrive at. I knew them well. The sleeves on his ʾ-shirt were rolled up to his shoulders, and he had the hard arms of a man who works outside in the summer. He was edgy, fiddled with a knob on the steering wheel the en-

6

tire time I talked to him; yet there was a softness in there somewhere. The kind of man who would break your heart and be sorry about it later. SATAN'S SINNERS was etched in purple on his right forearm.

"So, where you goin'?" he asked me.

"Santa Fe."

"No shit. Santa Fe. You know what foreplay is in Santa Fe?"

I leaned over and punched his shoulder. "You awake, bitch?"

He laughed, an interesting laugh with a touch of malice beneath the fun. Ex-con, I thought. State pen.

"Not bad," he said. "Not bad for a girl."

"I'm not a girl; I'm a lawyer. I'm going to Santa Fe to see the DA."

People like to tell doctors about their health, lawyers about their offenses. His was a familiar tale, beginning, he said, in Vietnam. A tour of duty brought out the demons: a heroin addiction; two wives in different states; arrests for this and that. Quality of legal representation poor, all lawyers shits with possible exception of self. Then down and out, broke and busted in Mexico, he found . . . the Lord.

"I've been clean for six years," he said. "I drink a bit but no drugs."

"Really? Six years. I'd say you've got it licked."

"I have," he answered with lazy confidence.

"Was it . . . the Lord?"

"He helped, all right, but I don't even need that anymore. I have friends who still go to church, but I don't need it. I just don't need it."

"What keeps you straight now?"

"Well, a couple of things. I'm going into business, and I got a good woman. I got myself a real good woman. She's a Mexican. Wanna see her picture?"

"Sure."

He pulled the snapshot from his wallet. Fondled frequently, it was wrinkled and torn at the edges. She was a beauty: big dark eyes, a cloud of dark hair, young and dewy—no more than seventeen I figured. To her he was probably bigger than life. Life is bigger than life in Mexico and at the same time, not worth a damn.

"She's down there right now with her family. I'm gonna bring her back soon."

"She's lovely," I said, "and I bet she's devoted to you."

"Devoted, that ain't the word for it. She worships the ground I walk on."

And what ground did he walk on? Red mud, from the look of his boots. Thoughts of Joe Feliz were pestering me like obnoxious flies. "I think I ought to give my car another shot," I said. "I have to get going."

"Okay, I'll tell you what: if you get it started, pull it over here and give me your card. I've been wantin' to talk to a lawyer. Guess it might as well be you."

"Gee, thanks."

"I'll follow you up the hill just to be sure it's running okay." I let myself out of the truck.

"Nice meeting you, Nellie, after all this time."

"You, too." I started to walk away and then stopped. After what time? And how did he know my nickname was Nellie? "Did I tell you my name? And it's not Nellie, anyway, it's Neil."

"I'm psychic," he said, smiling with snaggly charm and tapping his forehead.

Psychic. For a moment I had that watery sensation, a quivery blend of premonition and apprehension: strangers on a highway, one of us needing help, brought together by the cold hand of destiny. What would it all mean? Nothing, I hoped. Maybe it was a lucky guess; maybe I was beginning to look like a Nellie. All I wanted from this encounter was to get to the top of La Bajada. From there I figured I could coast easily into Santa Fe. The car started like a dream, as if the coughs and stalls had just been a put-on. I pulled over

8

next to the truck and handed him my card. He smiled, turning it over in his hand.

"You never know," he said. "Maybe I'll be seein' you again sometime."

"Thanks a lot," I said. "I appreciate it."

The car ran perfectly up La Bajada. He followed me to the top, waved his hand, and took off down the hill. La Bajada means "the dip." It's steep going up but easy on the way down. From the top of the hill you can see Santa Fe spread out before you, and beyond it the Sangre de Cristo Mountains, snowcapped till the middle of July. Santa Fe is a light center, they say; that's why so many artists live there. At certain times of day, the city is brushed with gold. It's memorable, but the trouble with all that light is that it darkens the shadows. On the way down the hill, the Rabbit stalled three times. I was able to coast long enough to get off the road again, where I waited for the dirty gas to recede.

Joe Feliz was no longer at the courthouse when I arrived. I figured he was at the nearest bar drinking away his disappointment, but I didn't have the heart to look. I went to the DA's office to reschedule the meeting. Demonstrators were parading in circles in the parking lot outside the building. Among the Mercedes-Benzes and four-by-fours, earth mothers and aging hippies with limp ponytails were holding up signs and chanting against WIPP.

They still have hippies in Santa Fe. You see them in Albuquerque occasionally, waiting lotus-legged beside the interstate for the magical ride that will take them north. It's a worthy cause, opposition to the WIPP project which would allow our government to store nuclear waste in a remote portion of the state, but this group didn't look like the people to be fighting it. They looked like right-brained dreamers in a left-brained world, worn out from fighting lost causes.

After I had rescheduled the meeting, promising that both Joe Feliz and I would be there, I went to High County Volkswagen and spent the rest of the afternoon waiting for

9

someone named Skye to get off the phone and change my fuel filter.

"Jeez, I'm sorry," he said. "It'll just take a minute." And then the phone rang again.

"You need help," I told him.

"You're right," he replied.

By the time I got back to Albuquerque the office was empty and still not clean, but there were signs that someone had been there as well as a pile of telephone messages on my desk. Call someone about a hearing in Clovis, call Judy Bates about her divorce, and at the very bottom of the pile a pink slip that said Carl Roberts wanted me to call him, ASAP, urgent.

Carl Roberts. The name left a lump in my stomach like a cold burrito. Carl Roberts was a partner in the "prestigious" firm where I'd once worked—a partner, and both more and less than that. Carl Roberts. What did he want? I left the message where I found it, at the bottom of the pile, went home, had a couple of Lean Cuisines and a Cuervo Gold, and got into the rumpled bed. The Kid had found his way out. By 9:30 the clock radio was set, the blinds were drawn, and I was drifting out there alone somewhere between the lonesome highway and the endless sky.

2

I TOOK THE car to the Kid's shop in the morning to have
him check it out. I don't trust people named Skye, but I trust
the Kid. You hear it all the time: Mexicans are lazy. It's not
true. All the ones I've known work, although they have their
own ideas about when. An appointment may mean something, or it may not; depends on how they feel when the ap-
pointed time rolls around. If it feels right they show. I don't
make appointments with the Kid, but I had an instinct he
would be there. He was, looking beat.

"Chiquita," he said, and put his arm around me. I leaned
my head on his shoulder. The Kid is tall, taller than I am,
although he's bony as a street dog. Actually, the Kid isn't
Mexican. His father is Chilean and his mother was something else, he never told me what. She died when he was
only six, leaving eight kids behind, and he won't talk about
her. He grew up in Mexico City; the rest of them are down
there somewhere needing money. He went to Volkswagen
school he told me the first time I met him, when I took the
Rabbit to the Sparkle Car Wash down the street from his
shop and water got in through a loose seal on the antenna
and shorted out the electrical system. I had driven two
blocks from the car wash, losing first my windshield wipers,
then the brake lights, then my directional signals. By the
time it shorted out entirely, I was in sight of the Kid's shop.
He put in a new fuse. I helped him beat a speeding ticket.
It was the start of . . .something.

"Yo fui a la escuela," he told me that day, and I spoke
enough Spanish to understand him. At that point the Kid's

English and my Spanish were about the same, a few spots of blue in a murky sky. My Spanish hasn't improved much, but his English got better and better. The clouds blew away and his mind cleared as the language came.

"You look tired," I told him.

"I play the accordion till three in the morning," he said.

I told him about the breakdown. "Don't worry, chiquita, I fix everything."

We had coffee and a couple of lumps at Dunkin' Donuts, and he drove me to the office in his pickup. It was interesting to get there late for once and see that the office *did* function in my absence. Anna was at her desk with her hair rolled up behind her ears in a new hairdo. Anna can braid her hair, crimp it, straighten it, or slick it into a bun. No matter what I do with mine, I look the same—shaggy.

"New hairdo?" I had to say something or she wouldn't have done a thing all morning.

"You like it?"

"It looks good on you."

Brink wandered out of his office looking harassed, a permanent condition. He could spend the entire day lounging beside my apartment pool and still look harassed. Now that women can be cavalier bachelors, does that mean men have to be nervous old maids? Brink isn't even forty, but you'd never know it. He's already losing his hair and gaining a belly. Soon his belt will disappear altogether and the few remaining wisps will no longer filter the top of his head. His eyes are small and of indeterminate color; they blinked slowly behind his glasses.

"How did it go yesterday?" he asked me.

"Terrible," I said, implying that I did not wish to discuss the matter.

"What happened?"

"I never got to it. Car broke down."

"That's too bad. I'm having a little problem with this pleading I'm preparing. Think you could give me a hand?"

12

"Later. Let me see what I've got going on first."

"Carl Roberts called again, twice," Anna said, eyes gleaming brightly.

"Um," I mumbled. Maybe nobody knew about the affair I'd once had with Carl, but everybody sure seemed to suspect.

"Listen, Anna, I wrote a note for you yesterday." I fumbled in my purse trying to find it; it was hopeless. I remembered what it said anyway. "This office needs cleaning, badly. You think you could get it taken care of this afternoon?"

"Oh, sure," she replied. "Just as soon as I finish typing this pleading and the deposition and the contract and . . . "

I gave up and went into my office, shutting the door. Carl Roberts. There it was, a pink slip, at the top of the pile this time. In all those papers on my desk there had to be something more important than Carl Roberts, and I rummaged through the pile looking for it. I took a few calls and kept myself busy until Anna buzzed me on the intercom.

"He's here," she said.

"Who?" I asked with a sinking feeling.

"Mr. Roberts. Shall I send him in?"

"Why not?"

So it was to be on my ground, this meeting, in the cozy nest of my own making: mahogany desk, potted plants, piles of papers. Carl's first trip to my office. He wouldn't like it. Offices weren't nests. Offices were places where business was conducted; desks should be kept clean and phone calls answered. His firm was run with precision and word processors. I tried to push my hair into shape. What was I wearing? A blue blouse, presentable enough, but there was a coffee spot on my cuff. Rubbing at it futilely, I looked up to see Carl filling the doorway, smiling like Burt Lancaster biting the air.

"Neil," he said, reaching for my hand.

"Hello, Carl. Nice to see you again."

"I'm sorry for barging in on you like this, but I had to see you and you weren't answering my calls."

13

"It's been a busy day. You know how it is."

I walked around him, shut the door, and turned to take his hand. Carl shakes hands firmly and efficiently. I did likewise. I noticed that his hand felt smooth and cold and that there was not the slightest bit of electricity between us. He looked fit, as always, muscles pushing against the sleeves of his suit jacket. He was wearing a light-colored suit with a pink shirt and a striped tie in coordinated colors. Rather pastel for Carl. He was, of course, tan.

"Been working out at the club?" I asked him.

"Here and there, when I have the time."

"How's the tennis game?"

"Pretty good. I played your ex-husband in a tournament last weekend."

"Really? How did you do?" Carl playing Charles. Carl *was* Charles, in megawatts. They say men marry their mothers and women fall in love with their fathers. Neither of these men was the least bit like my father, an eccentric, gentle man, but they were enough like each other to make me wonder. I'd gone from Charles to Carl like a crab in lateral motion, scooting across the sand. It was definitely not a forward step, and not my finest moment, either, but what did it matter now? The past was the past, and I intended to keep it that way.

"I beat him."

Of course.

"But it was a good match; tiebreaker in the third set."

"How is Angelina?" I asked him. She was Carl's longtime secretary, one of the nicer people at Lovell Cruse and the soul of discretion. People who aren't discreet themselves have to hire others to do it for them. He could afford it.

"Good."

"And Celina and the kids?" I asked him.

"They're great. Edward is four now, you know, and Emma is three. Looks just like her mother."

"How nice." Celina Roberts, née Esterbrook, was considered by many a beauty. Blond hair, wide blue eyes, long legs, good bones—a prize filly, nervous and dumb. Carl was in perfect health. He ate right, kept fit, but I noticed right then that some of the fizz seemed to have gone out of him, a certain lack of effervescence, like Perrier left open in the sun. Probably no one else would have noticed, but I did. Perhaps he needed a cigarette.

"Care for a Marlboro?" I asked him.

"Neil, you know I don't smoke."

"Mind if I do?"

He shook his head. Something *had* gone out of Carl. In the old days this would have been cause for a lecture. I lit up, sat down, and motioned for Carl to do the same.

"Well, enough about me. How are you doing?" he asked.

"Can't complain."

"Nice place you've got here." He looked around him at the potted plants, the papers, probably seeing exactly what he wanted to see: a mess. "What kind of cases you handling?"

I told him about Joe Feliz's DWI and the Bates's divorce. "And what are you doing?"

He mentioned the Sunlight Corporation case, a multimillion-dollar patent infringement suit. I told him I'd read about it in the papers. "We have an excellent chance of winning," he added.

Winning the Sunlight case ... I wondered briefly how many hundreds of thousands of dollars *that* would bring in.

"But that's not why I'm here, Neil."

I hadn't figured it was.

He cleared his throat. "As you may know, I'm running for the House of Representatives next year."

I knew. I'd read about that in the papers too. So that was why he had come. There was a pause. I puffed on my cigarette. "You needn't worry," I said, mashing the cigarette out. "*I* never told anyone."

"Neil, how can you say that?" There it was suddenly, a purple wound beating on the desk between us. "I didn't come

15

to ask you that. I wouldn't."

"I'm sorry."

"No, it's all right, don't be sorry. The reason I'm here is—well . . . " He reached into the pocket of his perfectly pressed suit and pulled out a dirty piece of torn paper. It didn't belong in that pocket; it was too dirty. It was like letting the street into an elegant room.

"What is it?"

"Here, you read it."

I took the paper, worn and crinkled at the folds like an old map, and opened it. Lettered crudely in pencil were these words: YOU STEAL MY BABY YOU PAY. The message itself was grim, but the writing was equally frightening: block letters carefully squared off, the pencil pressed down so hard you could see places where the point had broken off. It looked as if it had been printed by a disturbed child. It gave me a chill, and I handed it back to Carl.

"What does it mean?" I asked him.

"What do you think?"

"I don't know. A sick joke?"

"I wish it were. It's not the only one. I've gotten three so far at the office, always the same thing: a plain envelope marked 'personal,' postmarked Albuquerque. Do you remember, Neil, when we were seeing each other . . . ?"

"I'd rather not."

"I know, but it's important. Do you remember how nervous Celina was?"

"She had reason to be. We were screwing practically every day."

"Neil, please. We were making love."

"Whatever you want to call it. I was nervous too. Do you remember that?"

"Celina never knew about . . . you."

"It doesn't matter if she knew; I still felt guilty as hell. Besides, women know, they always know. They may not spell it

16

out for you in black and white, but they *know*. I haven't met a man yet who could keep two women happy."

"Believe me, Neil, that wasn't the problem. She never knew. The problem was that Celina was desperate to have a baby. It was making her crazy. That of course was one of the reasons things were so bad between us. You knew all that. It is so difficult to adopt these days; it would have taken forever. And then we found Edward, so we went to Juárez. It was either that or a divorce."

"Right."

"You know we couldn't have gotten a divorce. Celina's so fragile . . . my family, my career . . . I was up for partner then. It would have been a nightmare."

"Go on."

"Well, you remember when we got Edward?"

Perfectly. How could I forget? The bustle of papers and preparations, the trips to Mexico, and then one day Celina appeared at the office with Eduardo in her arms. The golden girl, the little brown baby; polar opposites and both so beautiful. Eduardo with black bangs and bright eyes, the kind of baby who smells sweet and doesn't cry, whose hair and skin are so soft, who makes you feel your arms will always be empty without him to love. They should have called him Eduardo: he wasn't an Edward. He was the death blow to Carl and me, although our relationship would have died sooner or later anyway. Shortly after that I quit Lovell, Cruse, and Vigil and teamed up with Brink to start Hamel and Harrison. Carl was made a partner, and in a few months Celina became pregnant with Emma, which happens often enough when people adopt.

"Why are you worried?" I asked him. "It was all perfectly legal."

"What's perfectly legal in Mexico? What does the law mean there?" he replied. "In my position, I can't afford a breath of scandal."

17

"Probably someone saw your pictures in the paper; the blond parents and sister and Edward, beautiful in his own way—but not your way. They're just trying to see what they can get out of it. Are they asking for money?"

"I don't know what they want. You saw the note: you know as much as I do. But there's something I have to find out. I want you to go to Juárez. I want you to talk to the lawyer who arranged the adoption and see if he is behind this. I never really trusted that guy."

Carl no doubt had never trusted anyone whose skin was two shades darker than his. And now Eduardo was his black-eyed son. It was probably the best thing that had ever happened to him. But how could he involve me? "Me?" I said. "That's a terrible thing to ask."

"Neil, you're the only one I *can* ask. If there is something, I don't want anyone in the firm to find out. I trust you."

"What about Celina? Does she know?"

"No, of course not. She couldn't handle it. Edward is her pride and joy. He's very bright, you know, and affectionate. A wonderful child. You can't imagine how much having him has done for her."

Oh, but I could. "What makes you think *I* can handle it?"

"You're strong, Neil, and you're a superb attorney. The best. I've always had the greatest respect for your ability; you know that. No one can handle people the way you can. Those cops in Gallup ... "

He *would* bring that up. That was how it began: Carl and I had been sent off to Gallup together on a case. One night he had a few drinks too many and ran his Mercedes into a telephone pole with me beside him. Carl's precision behind his desk has always been balanced by a lack of it behind the wheel. He couldn't afford one more moving violation, certainly not a DWI, so I climbed into the driver's seat and took the rap. I, who had never gotten a ticket for anything, got one that night for reckless driving. It wasn't a question of convincing the cops that I had been driving—I don't think they ever believed that—but of talking them into giving the ticket to me. They had to give it to someone. I was willing; I got it. Carl thought I was Wonder Woman, I thought he needed help, and before the night was over we were lovers.

"These cases you're handling—divorces, incorporations," he continued, skipping the DWIs, "it's a waste of a fine mind. You could have stayed with Lovell, Cruse, Vigil, and Roberts. You didn't *have* to go out on your own."

"Oh, Christ."

"I can afford to pay you very well."

"I don't need your money."

"Please, Neil, do it for me. It'll probably turn out to be nothing, and I need your help. Why don't I call you about it tomorrow?"

"Why don't I call you?"

"I'll call you." He leaned over and kissed my cheek, filled the doorway, and was gone. I sat at my desk with a yellow pad and listed the reasons why I should say no. I never wanted to have anything to do with Carl or Celina again. I am not a masochist, and besides, I had too much work of my own: divorces, DWIs, custody suits. They wouldn't set any legal precedents, they wouldn't bring in any six-figure fees, but they were mine. If I went to Juárez, I would probably get sick. It would be difficult, dangerous, scary. Blackmail, if that's what it was, was a matter for the police, not for me. Anyone might want to destroy Carl, but could anybody want to harm Eduardo, that beautiful child? It would be difficult, but intriguing. At least the outcome would not be a suspended sentence or a divorce settlement that no one lived up to. I might get sick, but I might love being in Mexico again. Mexico is crowded and extreme, happy and grim. Mexico is another country.

Anna buzzed me on the intercom. Judy Bates was on the phone, talking through tears.

"Judy, please," I said. "I can't understand a word you're saying." She lived in a trailer in the Rio Grande Trailer Park, worked as a beautician at Hairport, and was thin and nervous as a whippet at the best of times. It's a story I hear all too often: husband had left her for another woman. It would have been better if it had been another dog.

"Ken took Peanut. I left him with a neighbor while I went to the store and Ken came by and took him. You can't trust anybody anymore," she sobbed. Peanut was their baby. I hadn't met him yet, but according to Judy, Peanut was a prince among dogs—always shaggy, always affectionate, always glad to see her at the end of a tough day. Unlike Ken, Peanut didn't drink, didn't argue, and enjoyed the time they spent together. "It's not fair," she cried. "He has *her*, and what have I got? This." I heard a tinny sound as she kicked the wall of the trailer. "It's not fair."

"Of course not," I tried to soothe her.

"He says he can provide a better home. His new woman owns a house with a fenced-in run, and she has a child for him to play with. Peanut wouldn't have to be inside alone all day. He can't do that, can he? He can't just take my dog. I want you to talk to him. Tell him he can't take my dog."

"Of course not. But I can't talk to Ken directly; he's not my client. I'll talk to his attorney and see what I can work out. We'll try to appeal to his better side."

"He doesn't have one."

"Maybe his attorney does."

"Ha!" said Judy. "I've made a list of everything in the trailer that belongs to me, and that's everything. I want it all, and I've changed the locks on the trailer so he can't get in."

"What about the chain saw?" I asked her. "I understand Ken feels that's his, and his boots, his motorcycle helmet, and his Janie Fricke records. He wants those too. Perhaps if you gave him what he wants, he would return Peanut. It's worth a try."

"Oh, no. I want them."

"What on earth are you going to do with a chain saw?" I

had a quick flash of Judy Bates going to work at Hairport, chain saw at her hip.

"I just want it, that's all."

I sighed.

"Wednesday's my day off," she said. "I want to come by then and bring you my list."

"You can leave it with Anna," I replied. "I'm going to Mexico."

It was a trying day. Around five the Kid came by and picked me up in the Rabbit. I was used to seeing him on different ground—the shop, or my bedroom. Standing in the office with my key ring dangling from his hand he looked impossibly young and dirty in his greasy mechanic's suit. But the Kid has a way of tilting his head and laughing that makes you think everything will be all right, and as long as he thought so, I was willing to believe it. Carl was so impossibly rich and clean, but with Carl one had the feeling that nothing would turn out quite right, that he would always settle, settle, and settle.

The Kid went on ahead of me while I gave Anna some papers to type tomorrow.

"Who's that?" she whispered. "He's kind of cute."

"My mechanic," I said.

I got into the passenger's seat, leaned back against the headrest, and let the Kid drive. "It's been a tough day," I told him.

"Everything's okay with El Conejo," he patted the dash. "I gave him a tune-up, checked the points and plugs. He's running real good now."

"Wait a minute, what's that?" I asked. There, where the black hole had been, was a radio and a tape deck—and not just any radio, a Blaupunkt.

"It was lying around. I like the music," the Kid said. He turned it on. When it comes to music, the Kid knows one setting: loud.

"Kid, you shouldn't have."

"It's nothing, chiquita," he said. "Don't worry."

3

So I WAS going to Mexico. I prepared by popping a couple of cloves of garlic in the morning with my Red Zinger. It's not bad if you cut them up in little pieces and swallow the pieces whole. Supposedly, you don't smell like you had linguini with clam sauce for breakfast as long as you don't chew. They say it keeps the *parásitos* away; even *parásitos* don't want to live in a stomach full of garlic. *Parásitos—Giardia Lamblia*, amoebas—I had them all when I spent a year in Mexico deciding whether I wanted to go to law school. I had the grades but I didn't have the will.

Mexico was a balm: a mountain town with cobblestone streets, bougainvillea-splashed walls, serenades in the night, periodic trips to the beach in the back of a jouncing bus, and always the *parásitos*. But it had a certain charm then, going to the pharmacy, no prescription required, and ordering the drug that could cure your bugs for the day. Mexico, a lovely memory, always a possibility. I never forget that I can go back there and I follow the fluctuations of the peso the way other people watch the Dow-Jones average. If it ever gets to the point where I could live on a hundred fifty dollars a month again—if I ever have a spare hundred fifty dollars a month again—maybe I will go back.

"Going to Mexico?" Brink sniffed when he saw me on Monday morning.

"Juárez," I replied.

"That's Mexico."

"Not exactly." Juárez is a border town, not Mexico exactly, but not the U.S. either.

23

He wrinkled his nose. "What for?" he asked casually, and began drawing little rosebuds on a scratch pad on my desk.

"I'm doing some research for Carl Roberts."

"Carl Roberts?" If Brink had had any eyebrows, they would have buckled up like errant caterpillars. "I don't know why we need to take on work for Carl Roberts. Seems to me we have enough work of our own," he said in a tone that could be called petulant.

"Well, maybe we do have enough work of our own; maybe we're just not getting paid for what we do. The fact is, we are two months behind on the payments for the copier, the electricity bill is overdue, and we haven't even paid *last* month's rent." It was a low blow. Brink and I agreed when we went into partnership together that I would handle the business end. We both knew that he was incapable of collecting a dime from a needy client. That's why he needed me, and maybe why I needed him, and why we hired Anna to do the bookkeeping. But she wasn't any better at it than we were. Too busy combing her hair.

"That's not my fault," Brink said in a tone that *was* petulant. "You and I agreed—"

"Okay, I shouldn't have said that. But we never agreed that we wouldn't take on work for other firms."

"But Carl Roberts? Haven't you done enough of his dirty work? Don't tell me he's gotten a moving violation in Mexico?"

It was *his* low blow. There are some things you should never tell anybody, especially your partner.

"Why don't you go outside and water the rocks?" I said.

"Well," he sniffed.

"Look, I'm not going to do anybody's dirty work, okay? And it's strictly a one-shot deal. I am going to fly to Juárez, interview another attorney, tell Carl what I found out, bill him—at his rates—and that will be the end of it."

"I hope so," said Brink, shuffling off to the kitchen and the Mr. Coffee.

24

I had Anna call Licenciado Menendez-Jimenez, Carl's adoption lawyer, and make an appointment for Wednesday afternoon. She told him my name and where I was from, but she didn't tell him why I wanted to see him, and he didn't ask. Apparently it was sufficient that I was a gringa. He was agreeable to three in the afternoon, postsiesta, if they still took siestas in Juárez. She made a reservation on the morning flight with a return the following day. I decided to spend the night in El Presidente, the best hotel in town, and only twenty-five dollars a night.

I went to bed early, made sure the clock radio was set to KJOY, and fell asleep thinking about Señor Menendez and Carl. It seemed to me Carl was all wrong about this one, the result of a paranoia about Mexicans. I had done some research on Licenciado Menendez-Jimenez. He had been a famous divorce lawyer in Juárez in the days when divorces were a lot easier to obtain there than in the U.S. Now divorces are so easy you can do it yourself, but children are hard to come by, and you can't do that yourself. Women have fewer illegitimate babies, and when they do, they keep them. A scarcity of babies in America, a surplus in Mexico; Licenciado Menendez-Jimenez filled a need.

He got paid for it, too—up to twenty thousand dollars a child. An opportunist, no doubt, but I didn't think he would be behind the nasty business of the note. There was too much to lose. I thought a more likely culprit could be found right in Albuquerque in the form of someone Carl had wounded in his endless pursuit of the just verdict. There were any number of suspects who could fit that category. In any case, it wasn't my worry. I'd promised to interview Señor Menendez-Jimenez, and that was all I'd promised.

I fell asleep, only to be awakened from the murky depths by the scream of the telephone. A phone call in the night—that's when bad news comes, ringing the bell before it. But I was sleeping so soundly when it rang that I was talking before I was awake enough to worry.

25

"Hello," I murmured in the seductive whisper of sleep.

"Hi," said a man at the other end, no one I knew.

"Hi?"

"How are you?"

"Okay, I guess."

"Did I wake you up?"

"No, of course not." It seems ungrateful to let people know that they've waked you. I don't know why.

"I did, didn't I?"

"No, don't be ridiculous."

"You don't know who this is, do you? It's Sam."

"Sam. Sure, of course, I do."

He laughed and then I did know, a touch of malice beneath the fun. "Oh, yeah," I said, "the guy I met on the interstate. You never told me your name." I was awake enough by this time to light up a cigarette.

"Right. How you been?"

"Okay, I guess."

"Good. Like to buy you a drink sometime."

"I'll buy; I owe you one."

"How about later in the week?"

"Can't. I'm going to Juárez."

"Why you goin' down there?"

"I have some business. A client we're representing."

"No shit. I may be goin' down there myself this week. It looks like Maria is gettin' ready to come back. Gonna pick her up."

"That's good she's coming back."

"Right. Missed that woman."

"Sam, I got to get up early. It's a long day tomorrow."

"Sure, sorry to wake you. Be seein' you, Nellie."

26

4

I FLEW TO to El Paso, took a cab across the border and got to Juárez around noon. I checked into the hotel and had lunch on an outdoor patio with splashing fountains and chattering birds. Magenta bougainvillea splattered the wall, and the sun filtered through the leaves of a towering avocado tree made patterns on the floor. I ate something with beans, tortillas, and shredded lettuce. A señor wearing a white suit and Panama hat sat at an adjacent table and eyed me with sad longing, as if his heart would break if he didn't have me that afternoon. It's a performance repeated so often, you learn to admire the nuances if not the originality. He had a black mustache and white teeth, a diminutive Rhett Butler.

"Muy buenas tardes, señorita," he said, tipping his hat, as I paid the check and got up to leave.

"Muy buenas tardes, señor," I replied. In Mexico, at least, I wasn't expected to look like a professional. I wore a white suit and a lavender blouse, unbuttoned at the neck. Show a little cleavage in Albuquerque and you're considered a woman: untrustworthy. Mexico—already it made me want to discard the lawyer clothes and leave them in the desert like a used up skin.

I was ready for Licenciado Menendez-Jimenez at three, but he wasn't ready for me; still napping, perhaps. I sat in his outer office and waited, flipping through a copy of *Vanidades* featuring Princess Caroline and her babies and Jerry Hall and hers. I remembered Carl's parting words: "Remember you're not going down there to play softball." Around three thirty the door opened. Menendez-Jimenez came out wearing an expression of oily welcome. Sweaty and on the plump side, he was wiping his forehead with a white handkerchief. I noticed a ring with a diamond the size of a pea on his little finger. He introduced himself and sprinkled me with a shower of apologies.

"De nada, mucho gusto," I said.

"El gusto es mío, señorita." He shook my hand. "Come with me."

He led me into his office, which was not unlike mine: cluttered. Comfortably, I thought. It was done in new metal and old wood. He had a huge desk overflowing with papers and some gray metal file cabinets in the corner.

"You are from Albuquerque," he said, as if that explained something. "I have good friends there."

"Carl Roberts?" I asked.

"Yes, of course, I know Señor Roberts."

I got right to the point, "That's why I am here." I handed him a note from Carl, stating that I was acting on his behalf and that Menendez could talk to me freely.

"Señor Roberts, he is not in any trouble, I hope." His brow furrowed as he read the note. He lit a Camel and offered me one. I took it.

"Trouble? That depends on how you look at it. His practice is doing very well."

"Of course. He is very successful, no?"

"Yes. He is thinking of running for public office next year."

"So I have been told." He puffed at his cigarette and pushed some papers around on the desk.

"Almost four years ago, on June seventeenth to be exact, you arranged an adoption for Carl Roberts and his wife."

"I don't remember the date exactly, but I did arrange an adoption for him and his lovely wife. How is the child doing? Well, I hope."

"The child is fine. The father is worried."

"About what?"

28

"About this," I said, and I took the dirty note from my pocket and dropped it on his desk.

"What is this?" He looked at the note with distaste.

"Open it, please."

He opened it carefully as I had done, as if it had to be folded and unfolded along the exact same lines for the message to be revealed.

"YOU STEAL MY BABY YOU PAY," he read slowly. "What is this? I don't understand."

"You don't?"

"No, señorita, I do not."

"I gather that it is a reference to the child that Carl adopted through you."

"Impossible. Who would do such a thing?"

"You tell me."

"But no one."

"There's no one who knows who adopted that child? The mother, perhaps? Her family? Maybe they need money."

"Absolutely no one. Adoption records are sealed in Mexico." He smiled. "And to tell you the truth, señorita, once these adoptions are arranged, I forget. So no one has that information, no one at all."

"And you can't think of any reason *why* anyone in Mexico ... "

"Absolutely not." He paused, and some of the jolliness seemed to be oozing out of him. "Surely, señorita, you are not suggesting that I had anything to do with ... with ... this." He picked up the note with the tips of his fingers, as though it were a scorpion, and threw it at me.

"I'm not suggesting anything at all. I was just wondering what you thought."

"What I think is that you should look elsewhere. There are men in your country who are capable of such an act; I assure you that I am not." He puffed up like a bull snake, as if he could intimidate me with wounded pride.

"Well," I said, getting up. "I am staying at El Presidente

tonight, and here is my address in Albuquerque. If you have any ideas about this, Mr. Roberts would like you to get in touch with me." I handed him my card.

"Of course," he said automatically. He turned the card over in his bejeweled fingers. "You are so . . . pretty for an attorney."

"Not that pretty," I said.

Pretty enough, apparently. "Perhaps we could have a drink sometime?"

"Call me," I replied.

We went through the *mucho gustos* again and the *buenas tardes*es and I left him behind his palatial desk lighting another Camel. I don't think Mexico cares yet that you are what you eat and smoke and drink.

Well, the cards had been laid on the table, I'd done what I said I would do and I'd ended up exactly where I had said I would. Señor Menendez had too much to lose to be sending out blackmail notes.

I had dinner at the hotel—chicken with mole sauce and flan—and then I went into the bar to kill the evening. The room was dark, but sitting up there at the bar, soft as a moth in his white suit, was El Señor of the patio. His hands were idly spinning a glass bowl with a lighted candle in it.

"Buenas noches," I said, taking the stool next to him.

"Muy buenas noches, señorita." He turned, and the candle flame reflected briefly in his eyes before the curtain of languor and longing covered them again. His English was no good, my Spanish not great, but we got through the preliminaries. He was a salesman from Nuevo León in Juárez on business, of course. And me?

"A lawyer," I said. "I'm here on business, too."

"A lawyer?" he asked with polite disbelief.

After the second margarita his English improved remarkably as he told me he wrote poetry and, with great sadness, that he wasn't and never had been married.

"Y tú?" he asked.

30

"Me neither," I said, one good lie deserving another.

He sighed, as if he and I could make music from that out-of-tune institution. He did have beautiful soft eyes and hands that were never still. He played restlessly with a book of matches, striking a match, watching it burn, lighting another. I thought about it: his fingers fluttering on my thigh, the endearments in Spanish, the softness of his skin, his coal black hair, the heated fumblings, the embarrassment in the morning.

Saved by the appearance of a waiter holding his hand up to his ear. *"Teléfono, señorita."*

"Gracias," I replied. *"Mucho gusto, necesito salir,"* I said to my friend.

He took my hand. "Already? You are going already?" he asked, wilting in his white suit like a limp petunia.

"I must. It's a business call."

"Qué lástima," he sighed. What a pity. "You American women, all you think about is business."

"I'm sorry," I said. "I must go. *Mucho gusto."* I left him leaning over his candle, staring sadly into the flame.

I took the call in my room—Menendez-Jimenez. Trying to pronounce that name made me wish I had had one less margarita.

"After you left here I was thinking; maybe I might be able to help you after all." His fluency of the afternoon seemed to have vanished. Each word was pronounced with elaborate care, and I wondered if he had been drinking too. He paused. I waited. "There is some bad business, very bad business. If you could come over here I'd like to talk to you."

"To your office?"

"Right."

"You couldn't come here?"

"It would be difficult, señorita. It would be much better if you came here. Juárez is a small city. The wrong people might see me with you."

"I'll be there," I said.

31

I went out to the street, stood on the curb, and tried to hail a cab, cursing Carl for sending me on this mission, out into the lonely and possibly dangerous night with nothing to protect me but a series of T'ai Chi lessons. And would I be able to summon the Chi if I needed it? I was mad at myself for having said yes, for being here at all, but once you're in the river you can't stop the flow. I knew where it was leading: out to sea.

It took a good fifteen minutes to find a cab. As if to compensate for our paths not crossing sooner, the cabdriver drove with mucho gusto but the traffic got in his way. It took another twenty to get to Menendez's office. I thought about asking the cabby to stick around and wait, but that was a cowardly idea, and it was obvious that he was eager already to get back to the fray.

From the sidewalk I could see the light in Señor Menendez's window on the second floor. He had left the street door open. I let myself in and climbed the flight of stairs. My footsteps had the hollow sound of a watchman pacing an empty building. I got to the top of the stairs, turned to the right, and saw the light through the glass in Licenciado Menendez-Jimenez's office door, the only light in a long, dark hallway. I knocked at the glass, which was loose and rattled in its frame. There was no response. The knob turned easily in my hand and I slid open the door.

"Señor Menendez," I called. The only answer was the light shining through the partially open doorway to the inner office, lighting the slick covers of the *Vanidades* magazines, casting a long shadow behind the table on which they lay. "Señor Menendez," I called again, expecting a sound, a cough, a chair scraping against the floor. All I heard was the ticking of a clock somewhere in the darkness of the building. As I crossed the waiting room, the floorboards groaned beneath my feet. "You're an ass," I said to myself, "go home, get out of here." But my feet continued anyway. I reached the inner office, took hold of the doorknob, and peered

32

around the door. Señor Menendez was there all right, his head lying on the impressive desk, one eye visible and bulging, the blood drying on his neck, the diamond big as a pea glittering on his pinky.

"Menendez," I gasped. Motionless, I took in the scene, with the cold clarity of shock and thought absurdly of all the paperwork that had been spoiled by the blood, as if he were in a position to give a damn. He was, there was no doubt, dead, like a lump of a dog beside the road, and very recently, too.

I walked around the desk, being careful not to touch anything, especially anything with blood on it. I did then what I should and shouldn't have done—I opened the gray metal file cabinets. They were unlocked, the button at the top was sticking out, and the key was in the lock. I was still wearing my white suit and lavender blouse. I took off the jacket, and with that between my fingers and the handle, I opened the drawers, looking for Rs. Using the tail of the jacket I flipped through the manila folders. The names were mostly gringo: Ralph, Rich, Richardson—and there it was: Roberts, Carl Roberts.

The file seemed thin to me. I flicked through it quickly. There were some documents in Spanish, a few letters from Carl on his firm's stationery, various billings and scraps of paper with dates and numbers on them. I took it from the file cabinet and as I was closing the drawer I heard a slurping sound behind me.

"Who's that?" I turned sharply, my hand at my throat. I needed it now—where was the Chi? The doorway was empty, a pile of legal papers had slipped from the desk, spilled across the floor. It was no place for Neil Hamel, but I wasn't ready to go just yet. I leaned over Señor Menendez's already stiffening body and looked at his desk calendar for the day just ending, April 9th. There were several names that I didn't recognize—Garcia, Archuleta, Vasquez—and one that I did: my own. The entry that seemed the most interesting was the last one, *el perro dogo*. What did that mean? The dog dog? The double dog? This wasn't the moment to think about it, so I left Señor Menendez as I had found him, left the light on, left the inner door ajar, the outer door closed. I walked, not ran, the long blocks to the hotel, looking at no one, no one looking at me. I got to El Presidente, found my room key, went up the stairs, let myself into my room, went to the bathroom, and threw up the mole and flan I had once long ago eaten for dinner.

5

I SPENT THE night alone with the telephone, a standard black model with push buttons. Reach out and touch someone. Who? Another licenciado? I didn't know anyone in Juárez. The police? In Mexico you are guilty until paid innocent, and locked up for witnessing even a car accident. What good would it do Señor Menendez for me to be a suspect, stuck in a Mexican jail knitting sweaters for tourists? That's how they keep the prisoners occupied here, give them needles and yarn and put them to work. Menendez would be found in the morning with or without my help. I could call Carl, wake him in the night. People who live in glass houses shouldn't answer the telephone. I could call Brink, listen to him clear his throat and say, "Carl Roberts should do his own dirty work." And the Kid—if I could find him—"Don't worry, chiquita," he would say, "don't worry."

I turned out the light, pulled up the sheet, and tried not to worry. What information did Menendez-Jimenez have? Why had he been murdered? Had anyone seen me there? It was a long night, chasing those thoughts around the bed. But no matter how many hours I don't sleep, I'm always out when the alarm goes off or the phone rings. It was a jangling, jarring sound that the black phone made, and I was wide awake the instant I heard it. The plane didn't leave until eleven and I hadn't left a wake-up call: I knew that much.

"Hello," I said.

"Señorita Hamel?"

"Yes."

"There is someone to see you."

35

"Me? Are you sure?"

"Absolutely, señorita, they asked for you."

"All right, I'll be down in a few minutes."

I dressed slowly and brushed my teeth with a sense of grim inevitability. Who could it be but the police, and how had they found me? There are eyes in the walls in Mexico, eyes behind closed doors. I had a bleak vision of myself in a foul cell, knitting, fending off the guards with the needles. Damn Carl. He'd gotten me into this, he could get me out. Whatever it cost, he'd pay it. He'd have to.

I made my way down the stairs and into the lobby. It was, of course, the last person I would have expected: Sam. Sam, whose last name I didn't even know, was standing in the lobby, wearing a Grateful Dead T-shirt, jeans, and black sneakers.

"Sam," I said. "What on earth are *you* doing here?"

"Hi, Nellie." He grinned. "This here's Maria." Standing next to him was the young and lovely Maria, small as a child herself, with a beautiful black-haired baby wrapped up in her rebozo. It's practically the Mexican national costume, a rebozo with a baby in it.

"Neil," I answered automatically. "My name is Neil. How did you ever find me here?"

"We knew you'd be in the best hotel," Sam said.

Maria smiled shyly, unwrapped the baby, and held him up for me to admire.

"He's beautiful," I said. "Is it a boy?"

"Sure," Sam said.

"You didn't tell me you had a baby."

"Didn't I?" Sam kept right on smiling. "I guess I forgot."

Forgot? Would he forget he had a hand or a foot, a mouth or a brain? There were two ways to look on this visit. With one thought in my mind—to get out of Mexico—Sam was an unwelcome distraction. On the other hand, he was a diversion. I had two hours to kill before my plane left for Albuquerque. It was better to wait nervously at the hotel than

36

nervously at the airport, where I would be more noticeable. I invited them to have breakfast with me.

The baby gurgled placidly while we ate our *huevos rancheros*. He was a good baby and didn't require much attention. Maria was free to watch and listen while Sam and I talked. Her eyes moved back and forth as she followed the course of the conversation. Sam said she was learning English, but I don't think she understood a whole lot; her eyes had that cloudy look, the look of someone who doesn't understand the language. Sam made small talk for a while, and if I appeared distracted, I was. Every time the door to the restaurant opened, I looked up, expecting a policeman with my name on his lips.

"There was a murder last night," Sam said. The door opened for the tenth time. A businessman entered. If Sam was waiting for a response, he got none from me. "His name was Menendez-Jimenez. Someone slit his throat." He drew his hand slowly across his own throat. The baby gurgled and stared in my direction as if he wasn't sure whether I was part of the wall or not.

"Really," I responded.

"He was a very rich lawyer with ties to the States," Sam continued, playing with his knife and fork, tapping a tune on the table, his Satan's Sinners tattoo rippling across his forearm; a red sequined rose, a streak of lightning, and a skull on his black T-shirt; his arms tan and hard. "Did you know him?" All their eyes were on me; Maria's soft and quizzical, the baby's blank and unfocused, Sam's gone hard suddenly and brittle as ice.

"I met him only once," I said, not mentioning that "once" was yesterday.

"An important man in this town, Menendez-Jimenez. Lots of friends," Sam said, setting up a tinny vibration with his fork. "At least one enemy. He arranged adoptions for rich gringos."

"So I heard." I looked at my watch and signaled for the

37

waiter. "I have to be going. I have a plane to catch."

"They say some gringos will pay thirty thousand dollars for a baby."

"That's probably an exaggeration." I reached for the check.

"I'll get it." His hand slid into his pants pocket.

"No, let me. I owe you a favor."

He brought his hand back to the table. "Say it was only twenty-five thousand; that's a lot of money in Mexico. A whole lot of money."

I counted out the pesos. Breakfast for three in the best hotel—$2.50.

Sam took the baby from Maria and held him up. He showed me a tiny wrinkled hand and little fingernails. "He's very beautiful, isn't he? Look how perfect his hands are."

"I told you he was."

"You think someone would pay that kind of money for a little kid like this? You think a lawyer could set that up? How much would *he* get?" There it was again, that joking tone, the malice underneath it.

My patience was gone. "God damn it, Sam," I snapped. "If you're thinking of selling your own baby, don't tell *me* about it." I stood up.

"My own baby. Would I think of that?" he laughed. "Nice seein' you again, Nellie. Sorry you have to go. Give my love to Albuquerque."

"Thanks," I replied. *"Mucho gusto,"* I said to Maria.

"El gusto es mío," she took the baby from Sam and wrapped him up again, tight as a watermelon, in her rebozo.

6

THERE WASN'T A cloud in the New Mexico sky, nothing but thirty thousand feet between me and the irrigation arms ticking green circles on the ground. I called Carl from a pay phone at the airport as soon as I got in. The receptionist put me on hold and I listened to Lovell, Cruse, Vigil, and Roberts's Muzak play "Woman" while I waited for Carl's voice. Poor John Lennon, I thought. Shot down by love, turned to mush by Muzak.

Angelina, Carl's secretary, came on the line. "Neil, it's good to hear from you. How have you been?"

"I have been better, Angie, but thanks for asking. Is Carl around?" If she had any curiosity about why I was calling, she didn't let it show.

"He's on the phone."

"Do you think you could put me through? It's important, and I'm calling from a pay phone."

"Just a sec."

"Neil," Carl said, "you're back. How are you? How did it go?"

"Badly," I replied.

There was a pause. "I'm sorry to hear that." I bet he was.

"I need to see you."

"Okay. How about after work, say five thirty?"

"Not after work. Now."

"Couldn't we make it a little later? I've got a full day."

"I'll be in my office in half an hour," I said, and hung up.

The Rabbit was in the discount parking lot a half mile from the terminal. I bailed it out and drove to the office, struck once again by Albuquerque's Sunbelt charm; discount stores, fast food chains, one street just like the next. Anywhere U.S.A. but it *was* the U.S.A., and at least I knew the rules. I had been at the scene of a murder in Mexico, but I could not report it. Leaving the scene of a crime was a necessary but not a lawyerly thing to do. I wanted to know what had happened to Licenciado Menendez-Jimenez. I wasn't responsible, I wasn't involved—yet I was.

Anna was wearing her hair down. She has thick, honey-colored hair, and it curled against her shoulders. She had on plum frost eye shadow and was placing the last dab of matching polish on her fingernails when I came in. "Welcome back," she said, flicking her hand across the typewriter, drying the polish and handing me my messages in one economical gesture.

"Thanks. Is that all?" I asked.

"You've only been gone one day."

"A day? Seems like a year to me."

"You look tired. You all right?" She peered at me from under her frosted lids.

"I *am* tired, that's all. Carl Roberts will be here any minute. Send him in when he arrives."

"You got it."

I had just barely settled myself at my desk, gone through the messages, and lit a cigarette when Carl opened the door and walked in.

"Neil," he said, taking my hand. "Was it awful?"

"It wasn't fun."

"What happened?"

I motioned for him to shut the door. "Menendez-Jimenez was murdered," I said, getting right to the point.

"Murdered?" I told him the gaudy details of the crime, and he shook his head in disbelief. "His throat was slit? In his office? Jesus Christ. You didn't go to the police?"

"No."

"That's good. They are the last people you want to get involved with in Mexico. You don't think the murder had anything to do with—with the notes, do you?"

"Who knows? You're not the only client Menendez-Jimenez ever had."

"Were you able to find out anything before . . . ?"

"Not a whole lot. He said he had something to tell me. I was on my way back there but they got to him first. I took your file. It was all I could do." I handed the file to him.

"Have you been through this?"

"I glanced at it. Menendez-Jimenez told me the adoption records are sealed in Mexico—whatever that means—but I guess you already knew that. He said once he knew who the mother was, but he had forgotten."

"Forgotten? Did you believe him?" Carl asked as he flipped slowly through the papers.

"Who knows? I had no reason not to."

"Here are the court documents." He showed me some papers in Spanish. "No record of the parents on these. Here are some letters from me."

"Do you think anything ever *was* written down?"

"I don't know. It's possible. I know very little about where Edward came from. I didn't want to know. Menendez-Jimenez said the mother was a girl who got into trouble, a good family—of course, he would say so. Edward was healthy; I let it go at that. Did he indicate he had anything in writing?"

"He was vague. The file cabinet had been unlocked. It's possible something was stolen."

"There is something here," he said slowly. "It's not much, but it's all we've got."

" 'We?' " I said.

He ignored that and continued reading the papers. "Here are records of the phone calls he made." He showed me scraps of papers with dates and numbers on them. "He itemized the calls, although he never actually billed me for the time and charges. He charged me a flat fee . . . . These are out of order." He frowned and rearranged the calls in a way he found more suitable. "There, that's better," he said, handing the scraps to me.

There were several numbers in Mexico, some numbers in Albuquerque. Carl's office number was there, and his home number too—I recognized it, though I had never called him there. There were times, long Sunday afternoons with nothing to do, when I had gone to the phone book, looked up the number and then poured myself a Cuervo Gold instead of calling.

"Those are your numbers, I gather?" He nodded. "There's another Albuquerque number that he called, let's see . . . six times. Do you recognize it?"

"That's Peter Esterbrook, Celina's father."

"Why on earth would he be calling Celina's father?"

"In addition to owning a ranch, Peter Esterbrook is an importer. He buys produce in Mexico, sells it up here. He was my connection to Menendez-Jimenez. Menendez-Jimenez represented him on some transactions. Peter knew he handled adoptions and he called him for us."

"Say Esterbrook called Menendez and Menendez returned the call. That would be one call. Why were there six?"

"Perhaps they wanted to discuss it further." Carl shrugged. "I don't think it's important. Maybe they had other business."

"Does the phrase *el perro dogo* mean anything to you?"

"*Perro* means 'dog,' and *dogo* means 'dog,' that's all I know. Why?"

"That was the last entry on Menendez's desk calendar yesterday."

"I hope your name wasn't on there."

"Why? Do you think the long machete of Mexican justice will track me down here?"

"Probably not. The Federales are not known for their enterprise and ingenuity. Listen, I appreciate what you've done, Neil, and I'd like to pay you for it." He reached for his checkbook.

"I'll bill you," I replied.

"We agreed on an hourly rate plus expenses, didn't we?"

"Yes."

"Neil, that couldn't possibly compensate you for—for what you went through."

"A fee is a fee," I said. "I don't charge extra because the case turns out to be more difficult than I expected."

"This is a special situation."

"No, it's not. It's a case. I'll charge you for time and expenses, that's it."

"Nevertheless, I'd like to give you more. You have Anna prepare the bill. This is a little extra." He opened the checkbook.

"No."

"Yes." He wrote out a check for a thousand dollars in cash and put it on my desk. It was one of those checks with pine trees, mountain peaks and blue sky in the background. *Celina and Carl Roberts*, it said, *a thing of beauty is a joy forever.*

"No." I pushed the check back to him.

"Please." He pushed it toward me, closing his checkbook and replacing it in the inner pocket of his jacket.

"I won't cash it."

"That's your prerogative. I can't make you cash it, but I wish you would."

As far as I was concerned, I had done what I had said I would do and our business was concluded. I waited for him to leave; he didn't. He continued to sit in my chair, in my office, surrounded by my potted plants and papers, and I could practically hear the fizz fizzing out of him. It was his time and I intended to bill him for it, but it irritated me to see Carl sitting there flat as last night's leftover drink.

I waited. Waiting wasn't my forte, but I could do it when I had to. I watched him twist his wedding ring round and round on his finger. He was a skilled trial lawyer who knew how revealing gestures could be; it wasn't like him to fidget. In the courtroom his hands were subtle and aquatic, gliding and darting like fish. The air was the wrong element for Carl's hands; they belonged in water, in the emotional realm. I watched Carl once giving his summation in a rape trial. The jury hardly heard a word he said, they were so intent on his hands. His hands were the victim, pale, limp, crushed. The jury flinched as his hands acted out her humiliation. He won that case, of course. He won most of his cases.

"We're having a party this weekend," he said finally. "To announce my candidacy."

I shrugged. So what?

"I'd like it if you could come."

"I have other plans," I said.

"I got another note, Nell—Neil." His voice was low and defeated as he handed it to me. It was, like the first, folded and refolded until the creases were frayed. I opened it up. GIVE ME BACK WHAT IS MINE it said in the same block letters, pencil pressed down hard, smears where the point had broken off.

"They've changed their message," I said. "Do you suppose this is an escalation?"

"It's possible."

I handed the note back to him. "When was this mailed?"

"Yesterday, from Albuquerque. It was in this morning's mail."

"Well, that proves one thing," I said. He waited. "They *can* deliver the mail in one day." He was not in the mood for a joke. "It also proves Menendez didn't mail it."

"It doesn't prove anything."

"Dead men don't send notes."

"He was working with someone else."

"Why are you so sure it was Menendez?"

"I never liked the guy. I think he was a sleaze. I'm not happy he was murdered, but I still think he was a sleaze."

"You *think* he was a sleaze." Prejudice like that was enough to make me love Menendez.

"It's just a hunch, not something you can explain exactly."

"You're just paranoid about anyone who isn't as white as you are." It wasn't the first time I had blown up at Carl.

"That's an outrageous thing to say," Carl replied. "I happen to have a Mexican son who is extremely dear to me."

"You also have a Mexican maid; is she dear to you too?"

"As a matter of fact, she is. She's one of the family."

"Right. And how about the wetbacks your father-in-law hires to pick his chiles for a dollar an hour? Are they one of your wonderful family? You must really be fond of them—they don't even vote."

Carl's courtroom cool was leaving him. "That's a rotten thing to say. I'm not responsible for my father-in-law. You talk about prejudice; you're so prejudiced against me and anybody who has anything to do with me you can't see straight."

"That's bullshit. You and your stupid hunches. Are you making a hundred thousand dollars a year on your stupid hunches?"

"So what are you going on when you say Menendez has nothing to do with it?"

"I met the man, and like I told you, he has too much to lose and nothing to gain. Besides, he doesn't need your money."

"You think he didn't do it, prove it. You've got the means right there on your desk. Check out the rest of those phone numbers. Find out for yourself whether he was behind it or not."

"For *myself*?" I replied. "Now, wait a minute. I told you I would go down there and interview Menendez and that's all. No more. I want out of this."

"Afraid of what you might find?"

"I'm not afraid."

"Then do it."

"You're wrong, you know."

"Prove it."

Carl was so cool he didn't even smile, but he had fizzed right up in the course of our argument. There was a reason why he won all those cases: the manipulator supreme. Too bad he never cared about whether or not they should be won. Well, if he thought he was going to manipulate me like some inarticulate jury, he was wrong. "You fuck," I said.

"Please, Neil. You're a great investigator. The best."

"Not that great."

"I need your help."

I shook my head. "No."

"I'm willing to pay you very well," he replied, his hand going unconsciously toward the checks with the corrosive power and the insipid message.

"Why don't you get yourself a private detective?" I began to shuffle through the papers on my desk, searching for another project on which to bestow my great investigative skills, indicating, I hoped, that our conversation was through.

"I don't want a detective," he said. "I want you." His voice was so forlorn. If I'd looked up right then I would have seen a little boy sitting before me, his feet dangling from the chair. But I didn't look. I continued rummaging through my papers until I found what I wanted, the Bates file. He was not a little boy, he was one of the most successful attorneys in the state, a grown-up who knew exactly what he wanted. Just because he was capable of switching from lane to lane en route didn't mean he ever lost sight of his destination. Pleading, flattery, bribery, cool—they were the pavement on Carl's highway. I spread the Bates file out before me. If I put my skills to work maybe I could uncover the truth about Peanut. Was Judy giving him enough munchies? A soft place to lay his head?

"This meeting is over," I said.

7

I WORKED LATE that night, and when I got home I was tired, hungry, and thirsty for my old friend, Cuervo Gold. On a day like this the motel atmosphere of my apartment was just what I wanted. There's not much you can do to make an apartment with gold shag carpeting and fake stucco walls look like home, and I hadn't done it. There was the furniture left over from the marriage to Charles, a lot of newspapers and magazines falling off the coffee table, a small black-and-white TV, a cactus that had forgotten what it knew about water. It wasn't much, and I liked it the way it was. The office was where I worried about possessions, entanglements, screwed husbands, embittered wives. If I wanted to think about anything when I got home, it wasn't my or anybody else's furniture. Home was where I went to maybe be surprised by the Kid, or, more likely, be left alone.

I was alone, but I didn't feel like it. I'd been gone only one night, but it felt like my apartment had changed in my absence, like everything had been removed and replaced by an exact replica, like whoever had done it had just left. There was no sign that anything had been taken, but the atmosphere had been disturbed and the door to the deck was unlocked when I remembered locking it. When you live alone you notice things like that. I went to the kitchen, took the Cuervo Gold from the cabinet, poured myself a shot. At a moment like this, who needed ice? "It's been a long day," I told the bottle, "I'm glad to see you." I needed to go to bed badly and I locked up tight before I did, but bed wasn't any better. If anyone had been in the apartment, they'd been there, too. I fell asleep late, dreaming of light fingers, fat fingers, and diamonds big as peas.

I woke to a gray morning, wondering who had left an empty bottle beside my bed. As soon as I figured it out, I got up, dressed quickly, skipped the Red Zinger, and left for the office. As El Conejo negotiated Albuquerque's empty streets, I watched the sky changing in color from pigeon gray to dirty flamingo. At every intersection I had a long view of deserted streets and the thought occurred to me that I was the only one in town who was awake. That's the difference between old Mexico and new, old Mexico is always populated, always awake. Once the same country—Mexicans say they get along well with us considering that we took half of their country and the best half besides—it's the same terrain: high, barren, sunny, colder. But Mexico is never empty. You could climb thirteen thousand feet up Popocatepetl and some guy will be there with a box of Chiclets to sell. You could descend fifty feet to the floor of the Gulf and someone will tap on your oxygen tank and ask you the time. A Latin American poet wrote that the world exists only when someone is awake to imagine it. If that were the case, Mexico was being overimagined, Albuquerque under. Who would dream up this collection of fast food restaurants and perpendicular streets? Not me, although I might take responsibility for the mountains, resting elephants with a globe red as fire climbing the back of the herd.

In the face of morning primeval, my office seemed shabby and dull, but curious beneath the dull. There was the reception area: two-year-old *New Mexico*s on the coffee table, a wastebasket that needed emptying, a half filled cup of coffee with plum lipstick on the rim. There was my office: the potted plants, the window open a crack to let the vagaries of springtime in, the desk overflowing with papers, that looked like a mess, but wasn't—I knew where everything was.

I knew I had been working on the Bates file when I went

48

home but it was not at the top of the pile. I knew, too, that I had made a copy of Carl's file before I gave it to him, and that I'd filed it carefully in a stack of folders on the bookcase. I knew its exact location, but I checked the entire pile to be sure—it wasn't there. File R for Roberts was missing. "Okay," I said, "you've got what you want, now leave me alone." There was no one to hear me but the plants, and for all I knew they were listening. I shut the window—spring was on the horizon; I'd gotten that message—found the Bates file, and went to work. I'd finished a day's worth of divorces, a bankruptcy, done paperwork for two real estate closings, and gone back to sleep by the time Brink and Anna showed up. They found me, my head resting on a pile of manila folders.

"She said she was tired," I heard Anna whisper.

"I told her not to go to Mexico," Brink sniffed.

"Why not?" asked Anna.

"Shh, you'll wake her."

"I *am* awake," I said, lifting my head and rubbing my eyes. "Don't you two have work to do?"

"Did you spend the night here?" Brink asked, not noticing that I was wearing a blue shirt, not the gray one I'd had on yesterday. So much for *his* investigative skills.

"I got here early. I have an important case to work on: joint custody for the Bates's dog. It wears me out. Does Judy pay for the kibble, or Ken? Should Ken get him every weekend or every other? Who gets him for Christmas and New Year's? What do you think would be fair?"

Anna rolled her eyes. "Excuse *me*," she said. "I have some typing to do."

"No doubt," I mumbled, watching her detour in the direction of Mr. Coffee.

"You're so hard on Anna," Brink said.

"We *are* running an office here," I replied, shuffling my papers. Brink had been dismissed, but he hadn't noticed. Something was on his mind. He blinked slowly and flapped

49

his mouth, making me feel like I was outside an aquarium looking in. Something was on my mind, too, and I thought of telling him about it—the break-in, the violation, the missing file—but I decided not to. I was certain nothing of his had been taken, and I knew what he'd say, anyway: "Carl Roberts should do his own dirty work."

Brink cleared his throat. "Anna tells me there's not enough money in the account to pay the rent."

"We must have some outstanding billings," I said.

"Winter says he won't wait any longer. We're two months behind."

"How much do we need?"

"Seven hundred fifty dollars."

I remembered Carl's check then, lying in my drawer like a pack of M&M's a dieter leaves lying around just to prove she can live without them. That check was as good as cash, although I didn't intend to cash it. I slid open the drawer. It was still there, maybe it had been fingered, but it was still there, which confirmed what I already knew—the motive had not been money, and a thing of beauty is a joy forever. I shut the drawer and reached for my purse. "I'll cover it," I said.

"Thanks, Neil, I'm real short this month."

"Right."

"There is one more thing. Today is Anna's birthday."

An Aries. All that nail polish—I should have known.

"Do you think we could take her out for a drink or something after work?"

"If I'm awake we can."

For her birthday Anna got to choose the place, and the place she chose was Bailey's a singles bar on Louisiana. Bailey's was like all singles bars, full of potted plants and uprooted people and comfortable as a Mexican bus at rush hour. We squeezed our way in and I took the one seat remaining at the bar, entitled by my advanced age and my

50

having had an irritating day. The birthday girl preferred to stand anyway; it was easier to make contact. At the bar, which was large and rectangular, you got to look at everybody who was looking at you. Standing, you got to feel them. Anna struck up a conversation with a man in a red and white striped shirt and a yellow mustache about the Dukes, Albuquerque's farm team. What was there to say about the Dukes? They lost or they won.

I ordered a margarita—the first of a series, I hoped—from Sally, the bartender. Sally was a comfortable kind of bartender, soft and sympathetic, the way women used to be. She had brown hair that fell to her shoulders like a spaniel's ears, and flabby arms. She'd probably never worked out a day in her life, but she was someone you could lean on. Rarely as I came to Bailey's these days, she remembered.

"So, Neil, how's it going?" she said, plopping a margarita in front of me.

"Great." I began licking the first crack in a barrier reef of salt.

Someone sitting next to me was speaking—an attorney, of course. "Fuck litigation," he said. He looked like he'd been fighting the legal wars for too long, and the effort had left deep marks of erosion in his cheeks. He was talking to a young male who wore a sterling silver watchband inlaid with turquoise, a belt buckle to match, and cowboy boots that made him at least five six.

"I'm talking big," Young Male replied. "I'm talking City Corp. I'm talking Number One."

"Jeez," Sally said, rolling her eyes. "Excuse me. Duty calls." She picked up a bottle of Kahlúa and squirted some into a glass.

"I'm gonna make a mil by the time I'm thirty," Young Male said, "and you know how I'm gonna do it? Real estate," he answered himself before anybody had even had a chance to ask. "That's where the action is."

Anna, Brink, and Yellow Mustache continued to talk

51

about the Dukes, reaching over my shoulder and dipping into the chips and salsa, spilling wet sloppy chiles on the bar. I didn't partake. I like homemade salsa so hot it makes you cry. Bailey's comes from a jar and it just makes you drink.

I looked around the bar, saw some faces I knew and nodded, saw some faces I didn't know and didn't. A lot of attorneys, a couple of salesmen. There was the guy who'd tried to sell me a typewriter that never forgets. He had a Coors in one hand and the other on the shoulder of Jay Dean, unfortunate fellow, counsel to the despicable Ken Bates, slimy philanderer and kidnapper of Peanut. Okay, Jay, I thought, if you want to negotiate, I'll give you Easter weekend for two Janie Fricke records. Maybe the salesman had a typewriter that could settle: a trailer in this column, a car in that one, here a chain saw, there a dog. *Buy it, Jay.* I sent him the message telepathically across the crowded room. I'll get into technology when they build a machine that can transmit thoughts; this keyboard and memory stuff will be Stone Age before long. Jay got the message, but I guess he didn't feel like negotiating, because he smiled, shrugged guiltily, and looked away. Jay was playing, the Bates were work. Sometimes it's easy to tell the difference, sometimes not. Anna and Yellow Mustache may have been playing, but it seemed like work to me. Already he was asking her what she was doing later.

"Did you see that triple play last year?" Brink asked.

"Not much," Anna replied.

Listening to the dangling conversations and continuing my survey of the clientele, I was getting the distinct feeling that one of them was watching me. But everybody in Bailey's was watching everybody, glances roving around, bouncing off plants. Why me? I wasn't exactly at my best in a dark blue shirt with matching circles under my eyes. You're being a narcissist, I said to myself. Even narcissists have admirers, myself replied.

The faces at the bar were like fruit in a Mexican market,

primping for buyers, and I picked them over, admiring the fresh ones, rejecting the ones with bruises and rot. But that's what I ended up with, standing way around the bar directly opposite us, hungry brown eyes staring at me; a broad man with a fullback's shoulders, a chest to match, and legs that didn't. If his legs had been as powerful as the rest of him, he'd be a whole lot taller than he was. He looked fifty but could have been older; his hair was still brown and clipped close to his head in a menacing military fashion. His skin had droops and folds where even a sharp blade wouldn't reach. He had a pug nose, but that didn't make him cute. He was wearing a brown suit that fit like it had been purchased off the rack in some small-town cinder-block mall, but he'd be a hard man to fit, even in Hong Kong. He was wearing a white shirt with no tie—there was no neck to put one around.

My eyes met his—they'll do that if someone stares at you long enough—and he raised his drink, something clear, I noticed, no ice. It was an odd gesture, overly confident, or maybe not confident enough. There's a place where opposites meet, south becomes north, excess turns to lack. The place where weakness turns to arrogance is in the ego; this man was spending too much time there if he thought tipping a drink was going to win me over. For a moment there was a hole in Bailey's babble, no one chattered idly, no glasses clinked, no typewriters were sold. Nothing happened, except his eyes met mine. The sound came back on. He swallowed his drink, put the glass down, and walked away.

"Who's that guy?" I asked Sally.

"Andrew Monogal," Sally said. "He comes in here often, but that's the first time I ever saw him pay attention to anyone, man or woman. He runs the Mother Lode."

I licked the last bit of salt from the edge of my glass. "Where have I heard that name? Sounds like a singles bar."

"It's the gold mine in Lagrima."

So that was it. I hadn't thought he was a cowboy, or special either, even if he had been alone too long. The gold mine was a client of Lovell, Cruse's. I remembered that now, although I'd never seen *him* around the office or I'd have remembered that, too. "The price of gold must be down, if he can't do any better than that suit."

"Maybe, but the mine itself is worth nine million dollars. The government is going to pay that much to turn it into a nuclear dump."

"The WIPP project."

"You got it."

"That guy would be pathetic, even with millions."

"To you, maybe, but not to everyone. Money talks."

"I'm not listening."

"He's a lonely person, Neil."

"Who isn't?"

"He spends all his time out there with the rattlesnakes and mining engineers. That mine is all he ever thinks about; it's his romance, and his family too. You ever think about having a family, Neil?"

An empty glass was working its way across the bar toward the Cuervo Gold, Triple Sec, crushed ice, and salt. "Yes, but I don't think about it as much as the average human being or I'd have one by now."

"I think about it all the time and I don't have one. Every time I see a woman with a baby, I think, why her? Why not me? It makes me feel like I have a big hole in my chest."

"Baby envy."

"What else is there?" She took the glass and began to mix my margarita. "Work?"

"What else is there?" I looked off into the distance, out the doorway, down the road. "There's the lonesome highway and there's the endless sky."

"You sure you want another drink?"

"Maybe not." I felt a tapping on my shoulder, saw a glimmer of a frosted nail. Anna.

"We're going to the Wooly Bully. Wanna come?"

"Not me. You guys go. Have a good time, but don't be late for work tomorrow."

"Ha," she said. "Tomorrow's Saturday."

Brink was, as always, undecided, so I did it for him. "You wait here," I said, "while I go to the ladies' room. And don't let anybody take my seat."

The ladies' room was snug and pink, pearly as the inside of a conch shell. I let myself into the stall, put my purse on the shelf, sat down. The Mother Lode—what a name for a gold mine. The shelf snapped shut and dumped my purse to the floor. I bent over to pick it up. CHRIS IS A DORK someone had scratched on the wall, and JELLYROLL KILLED MY MAMMA.

Brink was in my seat conversing with Sally when I got back. She hadn't seen the triple play, but she had heard about it. Good old Sally, the kind of woman everybody wants to lean on. Maybe she'd make a spot for Brink.

"You keep the seat," I told him. "I'm going home."

"Already?" he asked.

"Already," I replied. "See you Monday."

Fresh air would have done me some good, but I didn't notice any. Sometimes the nights in Albuquerque are so clear you can see every distant star, even the satellites as they blip across the sky, but this night wasn't. It's the altitude that brings you closer to the stars and the mountains that hold the pollution in. The air was thick. It tasted like metal and smelled like New Jersey. I could hear the cars pounding on the interstate like waves on a nearby shore. I tried to remember where I had left the Rabbit. It was out there somewhere, bleached sickly yellow by mercury-vapor lamps. I started across the lot, slowly, walking underwater with the current against me. I was so tired . . . the lot was so big. I wanted to get into my car, put my head down, and rest. Even to think about driving home seemed arduous.

A truck was slowly cruising the lot, a souped-up number with springs that raised the cab a good four feet above wheels that were already four feet high. The body was black with lots of chrome trim, including smokestacks that poked like periscopes above the cab. A bunch of chrome tubes that connected the body to the wheels gleamed like vicious, shiny teeth. It was somebody's idea of macho cool, and it would have been laughable if it weren't so expensive, if it weren't so big, if it weren't picking up speed and gunning for me.

The springs weren't there just for looks: speed bumps didn't even slow it down. The headlights were as tall as I was and they singled me out. The horrible, grinning thing was going to flatten me. I ran. It was smiling, moving in. I stumbled, lost my shoe, ripped my panty hose to shreds, got up, kept running. I saw myself spread-eagled on the pavement like a squished frog. In the last second before it caught me, I dove and rolled across the macadam, pulling myself under somebody's four-by-four. As I fell I could see the thing swish its tail and disappear, parting a path through the haze.

8

THE VERY NEXT day, Saturday, found me in the office nursing my cuts and bruises, along with a body that ached as if I'd galloped a mustang to Denver and back. Lawyers in certain prestigious firms spend Saturdays in their offices—it's part of the mystique to work too hard, drink too much, have messed-up personal lives, and go home to neglected partners or empty rooms. That's what I rejected when I went out on my own. This was what I got.

I bent over painfully and picked up the mail the mailman had pushed through the slot. Among the letters and bills and circulars from Albertson's was a hand delivered envelope from Lovell, Cruse, Vigil, and Roberts, and inside, was a note from Carl: *Neil, in hopes you will reconsider. Fond good wishes, Carl.* "Fond good wishes," indeed. Where did he get such garbage? There were two enclosures: an invitation to his coming-out party on Sunday, which was not at his home but at a Corrales address I didn't recognize, and the file stolen from Menendez's office, a copy of which had been stolen from mine. Did this mean that I now held the only copy? It was unlikely. Carl kept copies of what he did, safeguarded what he had. Lovell, Cruse, Vigil, and Roberts were protected by an alarm system and a six-foot-tall Sikh guard in a khaki uniform and blue turban with a gun at his hip. The Sikhs, known locally as diaperheads, part of New Mexico's colorful community of religious worshippers, lived communally outside Española. Militant and efficient, they guarded New Mexico's more prosperous businesses, conspicuous by their presence, a reminder of who had something

57

to protect, attracting criminal avarice while they guarded against it. It's a valuable skill to cause a problem and solve it at the same time.

Damn Carl I thought. Persistent as rain, beating on people's heads, washing over and around them, undermining their foundations until he got what he wanted. The choice was simple: he wanted me in, they wanted me out. Scared off if I stayed out, manipulated if I didn't.

They weren't the kind of options you could line up on a sheet of yellow paper, draw a line between, and say this is good, this is bad, this is better than that. They were both bad. I didn't want to think about it, and the best way not to think about it was to think about something else. I spread my files out. Lots of munchies for the mind here. Judy Bates, for example; I owed her a call. I owed her a lot of calls. I had a stack of pink slips on my desk that said *Judy Bates called, ASAP, urgent, please return call*. She'd be pleased to know I was thinking of her on a Saturday afternoon.

What did I get for my trouble? Judy, in that state women fall into all too easily: victim mind. I happened to mention, casually, foolishly, that I had seen Jay Dean in Bailey's.

"You went drinking with Jay Dean?" she said, implying that I had been fraternizing with the enemy. She didn't understand one of the operating principles of the legal system, that men's club I belonged to—he wasn't the enemy, he was an adversary, and at the same time, a friend. That's the way things got done in the professional world.

"Not exactly. We just happened to be in the same bar."

"In the same *bar*?"

"It was seven o'clock at night. After hours."

"But you didn't talk to him?"

"It didn't seem like the appropriate moment."

"If you don't want to handle my divorce," she whined, "that's all right. I'll do it myself."

"Well, it's your decision, of course, but I can't honestly recommend it. There are matters of personal property,

58

records, chain saws, and a dog that seem to mean a lot to you."

"Then I'll get a *man* to represent me."

She'd gone too far. I took a look down the long, lonesome highway at life without Judy. No more phone calls, no more pink slips with her name on them, no more Peanut. "All right," I said, and started to hang up.

She began to cry. Her sobs echoed like they were bouncing off tin. I heard Tammy Wynette in the background singing about her D-I-V-O-R-C-E. That was self-pity. That was the chocolate cake *and* chocolate ice cream of self-pity. You couldn't sink much deeper into self-pity than that. "I just want you to help me," she cried.

"I can't help you until you turn that record off."

Click. She did it. "Now, where's Peanut?" I wouldn't have asked that question, except that I already knew the answer. As a matter of fact, there was a letter from Jay Dean in the pile on the floor saying that Peanut had been returned as a peace offering, now could we get down to business—chain saws, records, payments on the trailer.

"He's right here in my lap and you're not going to let mean old Daddy take you away ever again, are you, sweet thing?"

"Now, Judy, what you need to do is get out of the house. Take Peanut for a walk. It's not doing any good to sit around feeling sorry for yourself."

"Get out? For a walk?"

"It'll be good for you."

"Well, I don't know."

"I insist."

"I'll think about it."

It was good advice. I should have taken it myself. This day was leaving me with a craving for something; nothing as gloppy as chocolate ice cream or Tammy Wynette, but something. I left the office. It was a busy world out there. People washing their cars, watering their rocks, taking their kids to the zoo.

I got into the Rabbit. Saturday afternoon with no place to go. I just sort of released the Rabbit from its lead and let it wander. It circled up Central, then through the university and back out Menaul, definitely leaning toward the South Valley, the barrio, Callejón Blanco, the Sparkle Car Wash. It needed a wash, but that's not what it really had on its mind. It remembered how carefully—tenderly, even—the Kid had fixed it. This was something I had never done before, something I had thought I might never do. I had only been to the Kid's shop when the car needed work; never once had I stopped there just to see him. I found the street, Callejón Blanco. There was a line in front of the Sparkle Car Wash. Of the few things in life worth waiting in line for, a car wash wasn't one.

The Kid's shop was not much of an attraction, a gray cinder-block building with a flying-red-horse sign, surrounded by pieces of cars. I didn't see the Kid's white pickup, but it could be inside, being worked on. The garage door was open and I heard the sweet sound of Mexican music. Someone lay prone on a dolly under an old Saab. I could tell it wasn't the Kid because the Kid doesn't have big feet and fat ankles. It was his partner, Manny.

"Hey Manny," I called. "Manny."

He didn't hear me, the music was too loud. I tugged at his foot. He started and banged his head on something beneath the car. *"Puta madre."* This episode was beginning to have *mistake* written on it. Manny rolled out from under the car, not especially glad to see me, never having appreciated even my marginal presence in his partner's life. The Kid was the mechanic, Manny the businessman. He didn't like it that the Kid and I had something to do with one another. I was Anglo, the Kid wasn't; wasn't that reason enough to meet in the dark or not at all? His look when I was around was sort of confused, sort of hostile, sort of pretending that nothing was going on.

60

"He's not here," he said, demonstrating all of the above.

"Well, thanks anyway." So it was a mistake. I'd leave quietly.

"He's at his house. You know where that is?"

"No, but that's okay. I don't want to bother him."

"No bother. Here." He wrote the address down for me on the back of a bill. I'd never heard of the street, but I knew where it must be, deep in the heart and soul of the barrio.

"Thanks," I said.

"I'll tell him you were here." Friendly statement, but there was something besides friendliness in the tone. M-I-S-T-A-K-E was the song playing on my mind's radio. I stuck the address in my purse, went home, had a few drinks, watched a tennis match on TV. John McEnroe made a terrific return that went out. He threw his racquet into the net and called someone a fucking French frog. I fell asleep on the sofa, but when I woke up again it was still only ten. A women's volleyball match had come on ESPN. The room was dark, I was alone, I don't like volleyball. So why shouldn't I go looking for the Kid if I needed him? Didn't he come looking for me?

I got into El Conejo and put in my Patsy Cline tape. In twenty minutes you can go from mountain to desert in this state, from Anglo to Indian to Mex. The barrio was a bit of old Mexico here in New. Not necessarily a good place to be on a Saturday night if you didn't know what you were doing or where you were going; if you were a woman, Anglo, alone. There were long lines in front of the drive-in liquor stores—lines at the bank on Saturday morning, the car wash in the afternoon, the liquor stores at night. There are Saturday night brawls in this part of town, shootings, stabbings, by "Mexican nationals," as they like to say in the paper. I drove along at ten miles an hour, trapped between a purple lowrider out cruising and a black one. The bars here were bright, brassy, filling up. The Kid played in one of those bars, music that people drank and fought and slow-danced to. The music the Kid liked best was slow and sweet. The low-riders turned at the corner to cruise the strip again. I switched the tape to Willie Nelson and headed south.

In this old part of town, the houses are small one-story adobes, close together. The cottonwoods are bigger here—they've been around longer. Everything isn't out in front like it is in an Anglo neighborhood, where there is a street, a yard, a driveway, a house, in that order. Here the houses are likely to be right on the street, the yards hidden, and there are houses behind houses, houses down narrow potholed driveways. The Kid lived on one of those driveways, more or less alone, I gathered, but he had a lot of visitors; people looking for work, passing through. His address was 7 ½ Callejón de la Vuelta, a little street, an alley wide enough to get a car through, but just barely.

When I found 7 ½ I wondered if I was in the right place. The Kid's truck wasn't there. Of course; he was probably playing in the bar. It *was* Saturday. When you need to see someone, you never stop to think that maybe they'll be out somewhere. Had I ever been out when he came looking for me? He never said. I wasn't ready to cruise the bars, but I wasn't ready to go home either. There was a light on in the house and music playing. The song was M-I-S-T-A-K-E, but I hadn't heard it yet, and I got out of the car drawn to the light like a bug to a zapper.

When I got to the door, my hand flitted toward the bell, but I stopped first and looked in the window. The house was gaudy but neat. There was a sofa covered with a green chenille spread, and on it sat a girl stroking a cat, a cat with a thick, luxurious coat, a girl with an abundance of black hair. Like the Indians at the first sight of a horse with a Spaniard on it, I was so startled I had the impression that the girl and the cat were one creature. She was a lovely girl, a gentle girl, anybody could see that; a small girl, a Hispanic girl, a girl who didn't argue or practice law, a girl who liked cats, a girl who would be perfect for the Kid. I turned away from the window and went home.

9

THE BRUISES I'D gathered in Bailey's parking lot got covered up, more or less, with Revlon Natural Wonder. Carl's coming-out party was in Corrales. The driveway was marked by a couple of cottonwoods and a Hispanic boy in a white jacket who wanted my invitation. Some people make their statements with Sikh guards, some with Hispanic boys. I gave him the invitation and drove down the driveway, which was lined by lilac bushes that were about to come into bloom and Mercedes-Benzes that already had. I wanted to get as close to the house as I could because walking was still an adventure in pain.

I was the only Rabbit in a garden of Mercedes-Benzes, BMWs, and Saabs, but I noticed one battered beetle and I squeezed in next to it just to make El Conejo feel at home. Cars live forever in New Mexico; there's no rust, and no inspection either, but this one looked like it had run out of time, worn out, maybe, from all the messages it carried: IMMORAL MINORITY, I BRAKE FOR WHALES, and a sticker with green mountains on a white background that said SEMINATIVE.

The house was low and sprawling, white stucco with a red tile roof. It didn't belong to anyone I knew. Cottonwoods, which had probably been planted with the house, had grown up to shade and protect it. The house showed a blank face to the world: small windows, heavy carved doors, walls that were probably a foot thick. A Spanish house. You'd have to get inside to see if its soul, the courtyard, was blazing, flower bright. It was tended with love by someone. This was a lawn where water sprinklers ticked through the night even when there was a water shortage—especially when there was a water shortage. Already daffodils and tulips were in bloom, and the lawn was tender green shoots, too tender for the feet that were stomping them.

It was a balmy day, a summer day before it had even become spring. Carl and Celina's day, and there they were, the golden couple, standing at the head of a receiving line to greet Albuquerque's finest. Celina wore a white dress and high-heeled sandals; long lean muscles flexed in her calves. Her jewelry was golden and delicate, and her fine blond hair swung as she turned her head, smiled, and smiled again. At a distance, with the sun behind her, she looked almost transparent, like a glass of fine white wine. She was one of those blond women with a taste for pale colors, and she always made me feel like I was too much; too businesslike at work, too gaudy dressed up. I wished I had worn my white suit—anything but a bright yellow dress with a ruffle that kept slipping down my shoulder. I pulled it up and took a glass of champagne from one of the Hispanic waiters who wandered among the lawyers offering drinks that were invariably accepted. If there's anyone who drinks more than a lawyer, it is a doctor, and they were there, too, Carl's tennis-playing buddies from the club. I said my hellos as I made my way down the line, anticipating my reunion with the golden girl. There was a time when a meeting with Celina made me feel like a molded salad quivering on a plate. Today I felt like the bruised lettuce that's left there when the party's over.

Carl, smiling just like a man who is running for public office and not looking nearly surprised enough to see me, took my hand. "Neil," he said, "I'm so glad you could come."

"*De nada,*" I replied.

He turned to the little woman standing beside him. "You remember Neil Hamel, don't you?"

"Neil. Of course I do. How have you been?" She took my hand and I could feel her bones moving, thin as a bird's.

"Fine, Celina. And you?"

"Very well, thank you."

At a distance she was perfect; up close one could see fine fissures in the facade, wrinkles around the eyes, worry lines along the upper lip. Maybe things hadn't always gone well for Celina, but the hairline cracks were part of her appeal. They didn't make her seem older, just more vulnerable. Celina was not a modern woman.

"That's a nice dress," she said, "so, um, comfortable-looking."

"I like yours, too."

"This?" She looked for a minute as if she had forgotten which pale creation she was wearing. "Oh, this. Thank you. Carl told me you started your own firm?"

"Yes, with a partner, Brink Harrison. Hamel and Harrison. We're out on Lead."

"I think that's wonderful, Neil, but weren't you scared?"

"Scared? Of what?"

"Well, you know; going out on your own. *I* think that's very brave." She gave my hand a little squeeze. "Don't you, dear?" She looked at Carl.

"Of course, but we would have liked her to stay at Lovell Cruse."

"I'm sure you would." Celina smiled sweetly and relinquished my hand. "Have you met the children?" Edward and Emma were playing together nearby. "Children, come say hello to Neil. She used to work for your daddy." If this were a litmus test, would the paper be turning bright red now, or blue? Far be it from me to judge Celina's motives. Her eyes never gave a clue. They were pretty at a distance, up close a flat, pale blue. You could look right into them but you couldn't meet them. You could look right into them and not be struck by anything, not even embarrassment or your own reflection. I'd looked once; I didn't do it again.

Emma was a bland little thing with pale curls. She ignored me, absorbed in a cabbage-faced doll, but Eduardo stood up. "Hi, Neil," he said in a small, serious voice, as if he remembered we'd already met. He was as remarkable a child as he had been a baby, a little boy now, but still beautiful, dark, with black shiny hair cut into bangs and large eyes with thick lashes. One of those children who seem to come into the world knowing and sweet and clear. It never lasts, that quality of infant clarity, but it's lovely while it's there. If he were mine, I wondered, could I ever have given him up? If I had, would I want him back?

"Hello, Eduardo," I said. I wanted to take him away somewhere, somewhere he would be safe, but he wasn't mine to protect. He was Carl and Celina's. I hoped they'd be up to it. As he turned back to Emma and their game, I heard myself saying stupidly, "He's gotten so big. The last time I saw him he was just a baby."

"They do grow fast," said Celina. "Before you know it, they're up and gone. But it will be a while yet before Edward leaves us. Nice to see you, Neil. Now, if you will excuse me . . . " She turned to greet the next person in line.

"Thanks for coming," Carl said.

"It's nothing," I replied.

Leaving Carl and Celina to their long line of guests, I made my way to the buffet table, which was piled with fresh vegetables and dips, stuffed mushrooms, empanadas, chips and salsa, red chile, green chile, chile con queso, chile con carne. I helped myself to a mushroom stuffed with spinach and cheese. A nice mix of flavors, earthy and bland. But anybody can stuff a mushroom; parties in New Mexico are judged by their chile.

I selected a chip—homemade from blue corn tortillas, a nice touch—dipped it into the red chile, slipped it into my mouth. All quiet at first; the best chile is slow to light. But then my tongue ignited, flames licked my throat. There was the burn, the flare, the sudden clarity of vision. Delicious. I tried the green; even hotter, even better. Somebody knew their chile and they had a nice touch with flowers, too. The table was decorated with vases of daffodils from the garden and irises from somewhere else.

A man with his face buried in an armload of pink tulips walked up and placed them in a vase. The gardener, I assumed. He was dressed like the waiters in an embroidered white shirt, but there was a difference: he was white, too, the only Anglo I'd seen tending this party, about six feet tall and blond, with a bovine, soft-around-the-edges quality. There may have been muscle there once, but it was turning to flab. The shirt seemed too juvenile and too small for him; it belonged on someone younger, darker, firmer. His hair was in a long straggly ponytail that had been a mark of youthful rebellion once but was now a sign of middle age. He looked like a man who would prefer to live with his nose in the flowers, although he might fight for his right to keep it there.

"It's too early for irises, isn't it?" I asked him.

"Hothouse," he replied disdainfully. "The man wanted irises and he got 'em, but I told him the only *real* irises are the wild ones that bloom in the mountains in late May and early June."

"Hamilton Mesa?"

"You been there? Unforgettable ain't it? God's country." He rearranged the tulips and went back for more.

The music was nice, too. No seedy, leering mariachi band with white shirts opening over fat bellies. The band was a group of slender high-cheekboned boys who played music from the Andes with a sweet, reedy flute and percussion. Rather being a sparrow than a snail, I plucked a tulip from a vase and held it against my dress. A little gaudy, but that was okay; all the other professionals were decked out as cowboys and Indians. Concha belts, tooled boots, cowboy hats, turquoise and silver—it would be a costume elsewhere, it's a uniform here. But among the ruffles and fringe there's usually someone who stands out. Carl and Celina did, of course, in white. I expected them to. But someone else at-tracted my attention, an older man, tall, thin, prosperous, the kind of man who lived in the Heights, not the barrio, who drove a car, not a pickup. The kind of man I should learn to appreciate.

He was wearing a Guayabera shirt; nothing particularly unusual about that. What was unusual was his elegant bearing, the way he moved through the crowd with a slight stoop, as if he was accustomed to looking down. He was balding, but his head was so well shaped, it didn't make him less attractive. There was a snowy fringe of hair left, and a white mustache.

I watched him make his way around the party, looking on with amused curiosity, moving slowly, never letting anyone break his pace, a sleek greyhound surrounded by mutts. He must have been devastating when he was younger, I thought, but on the other hand, maybe he had grown into his appeal. Everyone has an age at which they excel. He looked as if he were peaking now at fifty-five or sixty, but that could have been happening for one year or twenty. Whatever, he had the aura of a man well pleased with himself, and if he felt that way, shouldn't I? I followed him as he circled the party, twirling the tulip in my hand. I think I peaked at twenty-eight, but there are moments when I can recapture the feeling.

He stopped beside a waiter and I walked up and placed my empty glass on the tray. The waiter grinned and motioned for me to take another.

"No." I laughed. *"Bastante."*

The older man turned and looked at me then, perhaps for the first time, perhaps not. I had the feeling he had already observed and evaluated everyone at the party and had taken no particular notice of me. Nevertheless, I was a woman in a yellow dress standing less than three feet away. His eyes were large and green, and he appraised me coolly. He had an interesting face, a fine bone structure, lights that flickered behind his eyes.

"Nice party," I said.

68

"Yes."

"If you like parties, that is."

"I don't, particularly."

"Then why are you here?"

He smiled slowly, showing perfect white teeth. "Because I am the host. Carl Roberts is married to my daughter."

I should have known it. He was as sleek and elegant as Celina was, but they moved differently. He was a greyhound who chose not to run; she was a filly who wanted to but was afraid, and the repressed speed came out as nerves.

"Peter Esterbrook," I said, speaking more to myself than to him.

"Yes." The unspoken question was, and who are you? But he didn't raise it, so I did.

"I'm Neil Hamel," I offered.

"Neil Hamel. Always a pleasure to meet an attractive woman." His eyes got greener as they focused on me. "Didn't you work for my son-in-law?"

"I used to work with Carl but I have my own office now. Hamel and Harrison, out on Lead."

"It's better to be on your own if one can manage it."

"I can. And what do you do?"

"I have various interests here and in Mexico."

"Mexico. Do you spend much time there?"

"A fair amount. I travel a great deal. I was in Mexico the week before last, then at the beginning of this week I was in Dallas for the Western Art Auction. I bought a small oil. I had some business in Houston on Wednesday and Thursday and I got back here Friday, which didn't leave me a great deal of time to organize this party."

Time enough for his secretary to call the caterer, the florist, the band. "I lived in Mexico once. I loved it."

"Once? You talk as if your life is behind you. Surely you're much too young for your life to be in the past."

"Not that young," I said.

"But so much younger than I, Miss Hamel, and I feel that

69

I have barely tapped the richness of life. Every moment is a golden opportunity. There is no 'once' for me, only the here and now as it becomes the future. I have no longing for the past. Do you?"

"Sometimes," I admitted.

"Have you been to Mexico recently?" he asked, crossing his arms and tapping his elbows with restless fingers. His hands were as elegant as the rest of him, but less in control; they moved to their own erratic beat.

"I was there this week."

"And you still love it?"

"Yes."

"Why, may I ask?"

"Oh, I don't know. I like the street life, the colors, the flowers, the intensity. The old people, and of course the children. The children are what make Mexico."

"They are *all* children in Mexico, Miss Hamel. You must never forget that. They are charming, but they are children. Treat them as adults and you will be sadly disappointed."

So he had an arrogance to equal his looks. Some people might have ignored it in deference to the looks. "That's an elitist gringo attitude," I snapped. "If you made an effort to meet them on their own terms, you might be pleasantly surprised."

"Are you saying I should become childlike?" His expression of amused superiority was beginning to look too perfect, as though he practiced it mornings in the bathroom mirror.

"What's wrong with that? Children have fun. They enjoy life."

"Maybe, but they have accidents." He was staring at a nasty scrape on my elbow that the makeup didn't conceal so well here under New Mexico's X-ray sun.

"So?" I said with a cavalier shrug that sent the ruffle slipping down my shoulder again.

"You should be more careful," he replied. His fingers, cold

70

as ice, brushed my shoulder as he reached over and lifted the ruffle back up.

"There," he said, "that's better. It was a pleasure meeting you, Miss Hamel."

"El gusto es mío," I replied.

Feeling every bruise, like an apple that has fallen from the tree and rolled and bumped across the ground, I watched him make his way through the crowd. When he was out of sight, I made my way into his house. I could always say I wanted to see the Western painting if anybody asked. The carved double door, about a foot thick, opened reluctantly onto a dark hallway, at the end of which was the central courtyard. I couldn't tell from here if it was blazing, flower bright. There was a table in the hallway and, above it, a small, very small, spotlighted painting: a couple of dusty cowboys, a lot of blue sky, a large gilt frame. I lay my tulip on the table—poor thing, already thirsting for water—and went into the living room.

Perhaps the interior decorator had done time in the Prado. The style was Spanish gloom. Windows and furniture were shrouded in red velvet and the ceiling was fifteen feet high, barred by dark beams. The fireplace was so big you could walk into it—if you wanted to—and a pair of crossed spears hung over the mantel. Don Quixote himself was standing in the corner, his shield at his side, and when I touched him, his metal bones rattled. I could understand why Celina always wore white and pink. In a room like this you didn't feel comfortable in bright yellow.

Heavy drapes kept the party sounds out but magnified sounds within the house. I heard a fountain tinkling in the patio, and then approaching footsteps. I stepped behind the doorway and waited.

The footsteps belonged to Carl. Peering around the corner, I found myself whispering theatrically, *"Psst.* Carl, I need to talk to you."

It's a mistake to interrupt a candidate who has just been

71

to the bathroom and hasn't put his public face back on. I startled him; his guard was down, his look was worried. "Neil," he said softly, not even faking a smile, just looking at me with surprise and a kind of sad longing. It was upsetting to see Carl like that, like coming across someone with their clothes off but their shoes still on. Not naked exactly—exposed.

"It can wait," I said.

"No, it's all right," he replied, looking at his watch, mentally buttoning up again, a candidate in a candidate's suit. "What is it?"

"Come in here." I motioned him into the living room, an appropriately gloomy setting for what I had to say.

We stood behind one of the sofas, upholstered in red velvet but hard as a pew to sit on. I told him first that someone had been in my apartment. He didn't believe it and he didn't even pretend that he did.

"Are you sure, Neil? I mean was anything taken?" Ho hum, was his attitude.

"I don't have much at home to steal, but something *was* taken from my office—my copy of your precious file. When I went in in the morning, it was gone." That got his attention.

"Are you positive?"

"I know where I put things."

"Thank God I kept a copy." Did I hear a "I'm sorry your office was broken into" or "I hope nothing was damaged"?

"That's not all. Some goon in a souped-up truck tried to run me down in Bailey's parking lot that night and came very close to succeeding." I showed him the scrapes and bruises. That got a reaction from him. Physical evidence usually did.

"That's terrible, Nellie, and it's all my fault."

I didn't deny it. "My name is Neil."

"I'm sorry. Neil."

"You're not the only person out there who calls me Nellie. Did you know that?"

He was absent mindedly running his hand along the back

of the sofa, against the nap, as if he were ruffling a cat's fur. "I didn't, but it doesn't surprise me that men are interested in you. I mean, you are an attractive woman. I've always thought so. And you look great in that dress, by the way. Yellow's a good color on you." Familiar he was in the uses of praise.

"I don't think whoever is interested in me is interested in my looks. It's something else, something somebody thinks I know."

"What could that be?"

"You tell me."

Carl was struggling in the watery depths; the signs washed quickly and subtly across his face. What I saw there was doubt, mistrust, and then the healthy sun-dappled sparkle of opportunism.

"I don't know, but there's a way you could find out. . . . I hesitate to even suggest this." His hand paused on the back of the red sofa.

I waited.

"You could track down those phone calls."

"I could get myself killed."

"Oh, God, Neil don't do that."

"I hope you're leveling with me."

"Of course I am." About as level as ten-thousand-foot Eagle Lake on a windy day.

"Then tell me what you've done to attract all this attention."

"Nothing. I've done nothing but adopt Edward."

But you've done everything, I thought. You've set criminals free, put innocents in jail. You've betrayed your wife and probably your lovers as well. You've represented environmentally destructive corporations and presented yourself as an environmentalist, and what has it gotten you? Power, money, prestige.

"Neil." He smoothed the velvet back down. "Do you think I should withdraw from the race?"

73

"Why? You're the perfect candidate."

"Maybe it's not worth it."

"Running away won't solve anything."

"Then you'll do it." He sighed with relief. "You'll check out those numbers."

"I didn't say that."

"I hope you will. It's important to me—more than important. It's critical."

"Before I do anything, there are some questions I want to ask you. Your father-in-law, for instance."

"Peter? What's Peter got to do with anything?" Carl began looking around him nervously, as if the walls had ears.

"I want to know his story."

"His story? He owns Esterbrook Farms, he owns racehorses. He's got import interests, export interests, communications interests, mining interests. You name it. Peter's involved. Celina is his only child. He dotes on her."

"Not that. What I want to know is, what's his story?"

"If you mean his past, he came here from Austria in the forties by way of South America, but he doesn't like to talk about it." He began smoothing an imaginary wrinkle in his suit in preparation for reentering the party.

"Austrian. That's funny. He doesn't have a trace of an accent."

"He's been here almost forty years, Neil. He's had plenty of time to lose it."

"Most Europeans don't lose their accents," I said. "They cultivate them. It gives them an edge."

"Whatever Peter's past, he hasn't held onto it." Carl kept looking around him as if Don Quixote were bugged, but I couldn't see what he was worried about: it was obvious that Carl wasn't the one to reveal any secrets Peter Esterbrook might have had. "He had a flair for languages and for business. It wasn't long before he started making money here and soon after he married Celina's mother. She was quite beautiful. Celina cherishes her photograph. She died when Celina was young, and Peter never remarried." Carl looked at his watch. "Look, I've got to get back to the party."

"Aren't you afraid that something out of Peter's past might turn up and harm your campaign?"

"No. It's been forty years and Peter has a lot of influential friends and besides I have no reason to think there's anything shady in his past. Probably it was just sad or traumatic. Peter *is* a deeply religious man, you know."

"No, I can't say that I do."

"Now, Neil, I must be going. I'll call you Monday. We'll talk." He began edging toward the doorway, but I wasn't ready to let him get away just yet.

"How does Peter feel about your candidacy?"

"He's all for it. I'm supporting the WIPP project and—"

"The *WIPP* project?"

"I can't be against the WIPP project in this district and hope to get elected."

"Why not? And the question is not whether you can or can't be, anyway." My voice was getting louder, but I couldn't stop it. "The question is whether you *are.*"

"There are pros and cons," Carl replied with infuriating patience. "On the one hand, it will bring a number of jobs into a sorely depressed area."

"It will bring a number of jobs into a sorely depressed area," I mimicked him in my snottiest attorney voice. "What about the long-term effects? We're talking about nuclear waste that's going to be lethal for thousands of years. Isn't that reason enough to be against it?"

"Not necessarily. Everything's not black and white, you know."

"Everything's not gray, either," I said.

10

THE WIPP PROJECT. Carl Roberts *would* come out in favor of the WIPP project, one of our government's more dubious efforts. There's a lot of nuclear waste floating around this country, by-product of nuclear power plants, the residue of making bombs. It's detrimental to the health, lethal for thousands of years, full of potential disaster in the wrong hands—in any hands. Nobody ever planned what they were going to do with it when they started making bombs or building nuclear power plants, but now the time has come to find these deadly stores of plutonium and uranium a home, and the home the federal government had chosen, apparently, was the Mother Lode in Lagrima.

It was relatively safe seismologically, far away from urban centers where more damage would be caused if and when something went wrong, and there were fewer people around to complain. It is a remote area inhabited mostly by rattlesnakes and mining engineers. Who cared about it? The Mother Lode—they stood to make millions, as nuclear waste is now worth more than gold. And also the town of Lagrima. They thought WIPP would turn their sleepy little one-saloon town into the Los Alamos of the southwest and put them on the map—if it didn't blow them off it. But once the construction work was completed and the construction workers—most of whom would have to be shipped in from elsewhere, as there weren't enough skilled workers in the Lagrima area anyway—had left, what would Lagrima get? Trucks rolling through, unloading their nuclear waste, drivers stopping maybe for a hamburger or a beer.

But Lagrima wanted it, they wanted the distinction of being the biggest and most lethal garbage dump in the country. It had to go someplace, why not where it was wanted? It was safer than most places. What did I or anybody else care? Maybe New Mexico was tired of being the garbage dump for the federal government. Sometimes you have to let them know that a bad choice, even if it's the best of the available choices, is still a bad choice.

Lagrima wasn't in Carl's district, Albuquerque was. In Lagrima they liked the WIPP project, here the feelings were mixed. Carl didn't necessarily have to be for the WIPP project to get elected in this district, but he did have to take a stand. He himself probably didn't care which stand he took. Each side had an interest, lawyers represented interests, all interests had valid claims, it was the one with the best representation that won. There weren't any rights or wrongs in this world, only interests.

I was at my desk drawing little diamonds on my yellow legal pad, filling in the spaces between the lines. Maybe someone was threatening Carl because he was the only candidate for the WIPP project, but why anyone would bother beat me. If Carl won the election—and he had a very good chance of winning if nothing unfortunate happened—he would probably talk loudly about the WIPP project on the evening news and do nothing about it on the House floor.

I took out the list of Menendez's phone calls, which I now kept in a file marked Auto Insurance in my bottom drawer. I looked at the numbers again.

Having been rearranged by Carl in chronological order, the first slip of paper recorded a call to the number Carl said was Peter's. It was dated April seventh and was twenty minutes long. I dialed it.

"Esterbrook residence." The female voice was careful, Mexican.

"Is Mr. Esterbrook there?" I asked.

"Not at this moment," she said, coached no doubt by

Peter. "May I tell him who is calling?"

"No, that's okay," I said. "I'll try later."

The next four pages were more calls to Peter, May eighth, May fifteenth, June third and fourteenth, three minutes, eight minutes, two minutes, fifteen minutes. The adoption took place on June seventeenth. What else had they talked about? The price of tomatoes, the ripeness of fruit?

On May eighteenth there were three calls to numbers in Mexico; three minutes, two minutes, four and a half minutes. Hamel and Harrison doesn't have a computer to keep track of our calls, so I wrote down each number as I called it, just as Menendez-Jimenez had done. I intended to bill Carl for these calls, time and charges. The first call was to a hotel in Mexico City, the next to a restaurant in Mexico City, the third to a hotel in Acapulco. Either someone connected with this case was visiting those places or someone unconnected with it was. It wouldn't be the first time an attorney billed a client for his own calls. Hotels and restaurants were not much of a lead, but every other week throughout May and early June there was a call, a few minutes in duration, to another number in Mexico. It wasn't Mexico City or Acapulco; that was all the number told me.

I dialed it. A very polite young man answered, *"Buenas días. El teléfono."*

I already knew that it was daytime, that this was a telephone. *"Buenas días,"* I replied, and then I asked him in Spanish whose number this was.

"Many people's," he said.

"But who? Someone called me from this number," I lied, "and I don't know who it was."

"Yes, señorita, it could be anybody. We are *el teléfono.*"

Then I got it. They were the answering service, *el teléfono,* one of those little offices with the green and white sign where gringos hang out waiting to place their calls back home. Since telephones are outrageously expensive in Mexico and the assumption was that if fate wanted you to contact somebody, you'd run into them on the street, very few people had their own phones. You made your calls from *el teléfono* and could arrange to pick up your messages there.

"Do you know the name Menendez-Jimenez?" I asked.

"There are so many names," he said.

I couldn't find out who Menendez-Jimenez called, but I could find out where. "Where are you?" I asked.

"San Miguel de Allende, Guanajuato, Mexico."

The state of Guanajuato, the *alto plano*, the high plain, the area the conquistadores loved most, and having spent some time there, I knew why. It was high desert surrounded by twelve-thousand-foot-high mountains, and it reminded the Spaniards of where they came from. It reminded me of northern New Mexico. The Spaniards built their most beautiful cities here, and San Miguel was one of them. Easter was approaching, the trees would be in bloom, the town would be celebrating Semana Santa, Holy Week, Mexico's most celebrated holiday. Menendez-Jimenez had called San Miguel de Allende every other week. Maybe Eduardo's mother lived there, but what prayer would anybody have of finding her if she did? Should I ask *el teléfono* if they'd seen a pregnant girl four years ago? Five minutes ago would be more like it.

"*Muchas gracias,*" I said to the boy.

"It's nothing," he replied. "At your service."

I'd done it. I'd made Carl's precious calls, and what had I gotten for my effort besides forty-five minutes of billing time? Peter Esterbrook—it wasn't any secret that *he* knew Menendez-Jimenez—one restaurant, two hotels, and this, *el teléfono* in San Miguel. San Miguel has an international population. Anyone who lived there might use *el teléfono*; so might anyone who lived anywhere else and happened to be floating through. Why somebody would break into my office to steal a list as unrevealing as this was a mystery to me. I found myself back at point zero. The only way to get any information in this case was to go to Mexico and bribe someone. I wrote down my time—one hour—including fifteen minutes for the aggravation—and then I called Carl.

"Neil," he said, dejected as a dog that had been beaten and whipped and then had spent the night in the rain, "I'm glad you called." That was Carl for you, high as a candidate on Sunday, low as a pup on Monday. I was supposed to notice this and ask how the poor boy was.

I didn't. "You'll be happy to know that I made your calls for you," I said, all business. "And here's what I found. There were five phone calls to Peter Esterbrook, three to restaurants and hotels in Mexico City and Acapulco, six to an answering service in San Miguel de Allende. What does that tell you?"

"Not much. What does it tell you?"

"That Peter Esterbrook killed Menendez?"

"That's ridiculous."

"Well, then it tells me that these numbers are useless and that whoever stole the file is a fool."

"There's got to be more to it, and you'll find it. I know you will."

Flattery, flattery—what did he want now?

"I got another note, Neil. It was in the mail this morning. It says . . . " There was a pause and I imagined him reluctant to unfold the note, holding it like an origami bird, hoping it would flutter its wings and fly away. " 'Get rid of the chick,' " he read.

"Get rid of the . . . chick?"

"They must mean you."

"No shit, Sherlock."

"Jesus, Neil, what am I going to do?"

"Do what I told you in the very beginning," I said. "Go to Mexico and bribe someone. You can afford it. You're wasting your time with phone calls."

"I can't go to Mexico in the middle of this campaign."

He could, but he wouldn't—not alone anyway, and not

with his family, and certainly not with me. Carl hadn't done anything alone since the day he was born.

"Right," I said.

"You could do it for me, Neil, couldn't you? You're good at that sort of thing."

Better than he was, I'd admit it.

"I'll pay for it, whatever it takes."

"That's not the issue. There is an element of danger here, you know. Certain threats have been made to my person. I'm lucky I still have my arms and legs, not to mention my life."

Carl was quiet for a minute, like a little boy caught red-handed at something. "I know that, Neil, and I'm sorry."

Sorry. Of course he'd be sorry—but that wouldn't stop him from asking me to go. There was another issue; maybe he wasn't quick enough to raise it, maybe he knew he wouldn't have to. The issue was would the "chick" let someone scare her off by writing notes? Would she let some scumbag threaten her and not even find out who?

"Skip it," I said. "Just be there with the money if I need it."

"Of course. You know I will."

11

ANNA GOT ME on a plane to Mexico City that left at six in the morning in the dark. People shouldn't start trips in the dark, they shouldn't get up in the dark. It's not natural. But Anna didn't know about that, as she never got up before nine herself. Since she was too busy to pick up the plane tickets, I went to El Viaje Travel Agency to get them. I asked the agent if any new method had developed to get from Mexico City to San Miguel.

"There's only one," she replied, "the bus from Mexico City. Have a good trip."

Mexico was a trip all right. Like taking a certain once popular drug, it can be frightening at first. There is too much to take in, too much noise, too much confusion, too many people, too many animals, too many short men walking around with long machetes. But after a while it becomes the norm, and when you look back at where you came from, *that* begins to seem like a dreamworld; menacing cars, hostile people, restaurants that pass out paper and plastic, space. One country is the other's dream—and nightmare—but which is day and which is night depends which side of the border you're on.

Mexico City had grown by several million since I'd been there last and the yellow cloud that hung over the place had dropped about fifty feet closer to the ground. If it got any lower the birds would fall out of the sky. It's an ecological disaster. The city's present population is about fifteen times the entire state of New Mexico and it grows every day. In New Mexico space is the constant, in Mexico City it's people.

The new citizens live in the hills in cardboard houses with open sewers flowing past the door. It's hope that brings them here.

A cab took me through the maze that was Mexico City. We were an hour getting from the airport to the building where the records of adoptions were kept. I tried to keep track of whether the cabdriver was deliberately wandering to rip me off, but it was hopeless; one street led to another and another and another. I'd get there when I was supposed to and when I did, the fare was only five dollars and the driver was impeccably polite.

The records building was enormous, the information stored there voluminous: births, deaths, adoptions, marriages and dissolutions of same. The hard part wasn't finding anyone to sell me information, it was finding someone who had the information I needed. Everyone was eager to please, no one knew anything. I was sent down halls, up stairs, past a computer room that hummed in a controlled environment. I sat on hard chairs and waited, stood outside offices and waited. If *la mordida* ever fails in Mexico, there is one last resort—tears. Waiting will do it to me, and tears of frustration were close when I finally connected with my informant. His name, he said, was Pablo. He was hidden away in a room full of files, a slender little man with a sharp nose and grasping fingers, very nervous about something, but not *la mordida,* the little bite. He was an expert on that. It's a way of doing business in Mexico, a payment here, a payment there. Salaries are low, the bite helps. A lot of gringos object to the system, but it doesn't bother me; you usually get what you pay for.

In this case, the bite was not a little nip, it was a gouge, but it was Carl's money, the place was about to close for the day, and I wasn't eager to start all over again tomorrow. I had worried about whether my Spanish would rise to the occasion, but I needn't have. As the Kid says, "English, it's the language of business." Pablo understood business. When I told him what I wanted and we'd agreed on the price, he scurried into his files and came out again, eventually, with the name Los Niños de los Angeles, the children of the angels, the church-run home for unwed mothers, where Edward came from.

"Many thanks," I said, "but I'd also like the name of the mother."

"Madre Mía." He slipped into Spanish, rolling his eyes toward the heavens. The mother was sacred, and none of Carl's bucks could pry her name out of him. "No, no, not the mother." He shook his head and began shutting down the office, turning off lights, burying files.

"Well, then, can you at least tell me where Los Niños is?" I asked, even though I probably knew.

"Of course, at your service, in Río Lindo, near San Miguel de Allende, in Guanajuato. You can take the bus."

It was almost dark when I got to the bus station. I took the first-class line, Tres Estrellas de Oro, Three Gold Stars. First class means there's a bathroom on the bus, a toilet in a tiny closet with a door that swings open to release the sweet smell of disinfectant and bangs shut because the latch doesn't work. A first-class bus is bigger—the odds are better in a collision. People don't talk to each other in first class, they sleep. Faced with the death-defying bravado of a Mexican driver, it's either narcolepsy or drugs. I mastered the sleeping technique, a form of self-hypnosis, when I lived here. I'd get on a bus, put my head against the back of the seat, and immediately go to sleep. I slept through skids and passes and thousand-foot precipices. I slept through the traffic in Mexico City and the mountains of Michoacán. I slept with babies crying in my ear and through pit stops with vendors pounding on the window.

It took a while to get used to the bouncing bus, the banging door, the disinfectant smell, the ai-yai-yai-yai music, but by eight we were out of Mexico City. I pressed my face into the upholstery and went to sleep. Near midnight I woke in

84

San Miguel. Even in the middle of the night climbing out of an idling bus with diesel fumes in my face, it had charm. The gaslights lit cobblestone streets, pastel walls, carved doors. The night was so clear you could see every remote star.

I found a taxi and the driver took me to a hotel near the Paroquia, San Miguel's gingerbread cathedral modeled on a postcard someone saw of a cathedral in Europe, but mangled in the translation. The hotel had a medieval door, heavy enough to guard a moat. I pounded until somebody woke up and let me in. As soon as I found a room my head fell onto the pillow and I went to sleep. It felt a whole lot better than Three Gold Stars' plastic upholstery. When I woke up, it seemed like I was dreaming of Mexico, but the quality of the air, the smell of woodsmoke, the singing birds said it was the real thing, not Juárez, not Mexico City even: Mexico. I dressed in running shoes and jeans for the day's investigation, had a *bolio* and fresh squeezed orange juice in the hotel's patio, and watched a bougainvillea climb the wall. Mexico.

The hotel was only a short walk to the jardín, San Miguel's plaza. It was an especially green plaza. The trees were clipped flat as a table on top and dense underneath. In the evening the birds fly in from the desert, turn in unison, and drop into the trees.

El teléfono is on Angulo, which means "elbow." There is a *tortillería* on Angulo, a place where a machine mashes down corn and pops out tortillas, where local señoras buy them warm by the kilo wrapped in newspaper. A truck was parked in front of the *tortillería* unloading hundred-pound sacks of corn. The driver dropped one and it broke, spilling corn kernels all over the street.

"Puta madre," he said. Your mother is a whore.

"It's nothing," the *tortillería* owner replied. He came out with a broom and swept it all up—the corn, the dog shit, the burro droppings, the gum wrappers and anything else

85

that happened to be in the street—took it inside and fed it to the hungry tortilla machine. Mexico.

Elbow was a good name for the crooked street, or maybe ankle. It would have been easy to break one climbing over the cobblestones. I was glad I had my running shoes on. I saw the green and white sign, EL TELÉFONO. When I lived in Mexico a private *teléfono* cost five hundred dollars just to install, a year's salary for some. If you wanted to talk to someone, you just hung out in the plaza and sooner or later they showed up. Sometimes now I'd pay five hundred dollars to get rid of mine. There were sounds you were glad you were rid of here: ringing telephones, airplanes—if an airplane flew over San Miguel it was an event; there were others you could do without: the barking dogs, the turkeys that gobbled all night.

Already gringos were lined up waiting for the phone: an older man in a lithium slump reading a dated *Wall Street Journal*, one of San Miguel's population of dedicated drinkers and casualties of war; two girls dressed in *huipils* and *huaraches* from the floating population of tourists. I went right up to the desk. *"Buenas días,"* I said.

Two teenage boys were sitting there reading comic books and chewing Chiclets, polite as only Mexican boys can be.

"Buenas días," they replied.

Hoping to get more information about the place, I asked them if they were the answering service for Los Niños de los Angeles. The boys looked at each other. They were the same type, wiry and amused, brothers, probably, or cousins.

"Río Lindo," one said.

"La Iglesia," said the other.

"La Rubia," they both said and began to giggle.

La Rubia, the blonde, a person you see a lot of in Mexico selling beer and cigarettes. Certainly not me.

"Who is La Rubia?" I asked.

"She is ... " one began.

"La Rubia," the other finished, and they giggled some more.

"She's at Río Lindo?"

"Absolutely," they replied.

12

THERE WAS ONLY one bus to Río Lindo, third class or worse, a faded blue wreck with battered fenders, fringe in the windows, and tires that were smooth as silk. Drivers in Mexico take a personal interest in their buses, decorating and embellishing them just like home. Some of them paint names on the bumper or inspiring sayings such as this one had: SOLO DIO SABE MÍ FIN, Only God Knows My End. A plastic Jesus bobbled on the dash, a fitting companion for the journey to Los Niños de los Angeles. The seats were blue plastic, with holes to let the foam rubber stuffing breathe. It had taken a deep breath and run away. The backs were yellow metal, straight up and pint-size. The only way to sleep here would be with your head dangling back like a baby's.

A woman wearing the ubiquitous black and white rebozo sat down next to me, cradling a baby goat in her arms. A boy tried to lure his piglet through the aisle. When persuasion didn't work he shouted *"Maricón"* and gave it a good kick. Oink you, the piglet replied. Someone put a crate of squawking chickens on the roof. When we were fully loaded, we set off, radio blaring, springs squeaking, pig oinking, driver yelling, *"Celaya, Celay-a."* Only God knew if it was his destination.

Once we left San Miguel the countryside became desert very rapidly. At a distance the town was an oasis, green and inviting, but the country around it was as barren as the moon, except for the papers that littered the roadside, an occasional cactus, and the people walking or standing beside the road in their rebozos and plastic sombreros. The bus stopped frequently, people got off and on where there was nothing to mark the spot. The driver stopped calling out the names; maybe there were too many, maybe there were none. Finally, at one of the stops, the woman next to me leaned over and whispered, *"Río Lindo."* She smiled mysteriously as if she knew all the secrets of that place, including why I was going there. *"Gracias,"* I said, climbing over her. She held the goat up to let me pass and it baaed sweetly.

A young girl got off with me. She was probably no more than sixteen and very pregnant. She had a lovely smile and dreamy eyes, one of those girls who glow when they are with child. The bus bounced out of sight and we were left together beside the highway. A dirt road curved around nothing and led to nowhere and a small hand lettered arrow said RÍO LINDO.

"Tú vas a Río Lindo?" I asked the girl. You are going to Río Lindo?

"Sí," she said, smiling, her hand unconsciously rubbing her belly. She had the kind of placidity that could give you confidence in a strange place, and this place was as strange as any, a home for unwed mothers on the face of the moon. Mexican women have been raised for centuries to be helpful, and no one does it better. The men may still have the power, but they've had it for too long: it's turned them into drunkards and flakes. It's the women who hold things together. The girl had an ethereal face, but she wore sensible shoes, clunky black loafers. She began walking with no hesitation in the direction of the arrow. I followed, glad I had on my running shoes. My cleat marks, I noticed, were not the only ones in the road.

The girl answered my questions. Her name was Mercedes, she said. She was going to the church and would be pleased to take me with her. She was polite, but it was clear she wanted to save her energy for walking, so we continued in silence, the sun directly above our heads, the dust at our feet, nagged by a black crow that circled and squawked. Everything matters, it crowed, and nothing.

The church at Río Lindo was a tiny white chapel. It looked like a mushroom that had sprung up, had its moment in the sun, and was sinking back into the ground again. It was shaded by a large tree and was not far from the banks of the mighty Río Lindo, six inches of stagnant brown water surrounded by a dry riverbed that was littered with scrap paper and Orange Fanta bottles.

As we approached I heard music drifting from the open doorway of the chapel. "Wait here," the girl said in Spanish, smiling graciously. "The pastor will see you." She disappeared down the dusty road. The music was an organ, sounding just like the organs I heard at church when I was a child—out of tune. A man was singing, *"What a friend we have in Jesus, all our sins and griefs to bear. What a privilege to carry everything to God in prayer."* When he finished he began to speak: a sermon, I gathered. His voice was loud and self-conscious, the voice of someone who is used to not being heard but who persists anyway. At first I thought he was speaking English, but it was Spanish, more or less, to an English beat. The words had something to do with God loving children and wanting the best for them. I sat down on the steps and waited for him to finish. A skinny three-legged dog lay on the ground watching the fleas climbing its legs, too lazy even to nip. At the end of the sermon, the man said, "Jesus loves you and he loves your unborn child. God bless you." He gave the benediction, and exit music began to play.

About fifteen girls came out of the chapel, pregnant, every one of them, *embarazado,* but not embarrassed. Superficially they were alike, dark skinned with shining black hair, bright as flowers in their cheap clothes, but on closer examination each one was unique. Some smiled shyly and wished me a good day, some had that placid glow that comes in the later stages of pregnancy, some were thin and hardly showed, some had the pregnant woman's waddle. Coming upon the whole group of them in this barren place was like finding a tree in the middle of the desert dripping ripe

90

squishy fruit. Mexico overwhelmed me once again. Endless children and animals and flowers springing from dry river-beds and dust. It's the country's joy and its curse; there are not enough jobs to support this life, not enough food to feed it. One of the laws that governs human behavior is that the less people have the more they reproduce. The one way to stop overpopulation is to make everybody rich, or at least comfortable. Maybe this place was doing a service by shipping babies to Gringolandia, where there was an excess of food, a paucity of children, but it was a decision I wouldn't want to make. Mexican women don't give up their children lightly. There's a long tradition to have them and keep them despite the odds. How many of them had made the decision and then wanted the child back? Eduardo's mother could be a girl just like one of these, who wasn't able to have any more children. Or maybe she just changed her mind.

There were a couple of metal buildings down the road from the chapel, and the girls headed in that direction. The dog pulled himself to his three feet and followed. The organ continued to play. I got up and looked inside the chapel; it was as simple as the outside, white with wooden pews, the only decoration being a plain wooden cross above the altar: no candles, no statues of virgins dripping lace and Jesuses dripping blood, no *retablos* celebrating miracles of divine intervention, no bunches of manzanita or mint. The walls were absolutely white. I wondered what the girls thought about practicing religion in a whitewashed chapel, but then they probably weren't practicing religion, considering the minister's Spanish. It was probably just a duty to perform on the way to giving up their children.

The minister had a mirror on top of the organ that focused on the doorway. I must have appeared in it, because he stopped playing suddenly and turned around. "Hello," he said, standing up to greet me. He was medium-size with wiry gray hair, the kind of hair that's out of control no matter what you do to it, but I didn't think he did much. He had pale, dis-

91

tracted eyes and a worn, rivuleted face, the sort of I-need-you face that has a romantic appeal when you are too young to know better.

"Sometimes I stay here just to play a while," he said shyly, embarrassed to be caught at it. "We don't get many visitors at Río Lindo. I'm Henry."

"Neil Hamel," I replied. "You're not so easy to get to."

"That's true." He smiled, proving he was glad to see me, but he never looked at me as we talked, only at a point about three inches to the side of my head. A case of do-good burnout, I figured. People who spend too much time trying to help others reach a point where they don't look or listen anymore. There's probably a limited number of people you can care about in a lifetime, and when that number has been reached, it's over. I've seen it happen in all the people professions: to social workers, teachers, nurses, even occasionally to a lawyer. The next step is usually drink, and I could see he'd taken it. A fine fuschia network marked his cheeks, and his hand shook as he reached for mine. His breath smelled like maguey mold. We talked about the chapel and the girls and what he expected to accomplish, which was putting unwanted babies in good homes, of course. He was a very sweet shell of a man, eager to talk. He didn't seem to care why I was there. He asked me if I'd like to take a look around the place and I accepted.

We began with the dorm, a metal building that would be hotter than Tucson in the summertime and wasn't exactly comfortable now. There was a row of beds covered with cotton spreads on each side of the room. It looked like a barracks, except that each girl had pasted pictures and mementos above her bed. A radio on the floor was blaring something about *amor*. The girls were all in the commissary having lunch, and we went there next. They sat at long tables with white tablecloths eating cottage cheese and canned peaches on a bed of iceberg lettuce.

"No beans and tortillas?" I asked.

92

"Leona, my wife, is in charge of the menus. She's a trained dietician," Henry said.

A radio was blaring the same song, *"Amor, amor, amor."* I guess the girls were true believers. They *were* girls, too, that was no euphemism, each of them was so young. Some looked up from their cottage cheese and smiled shyly at me, as if they thought I might be there to take one of their babies. I couldn't help myself, I smiled back.

"Let's see." Henry wrinkled up his forehead. "What else? There's the delivery room." We left the girls to the diet special and he took me there next, a shiny sterile room with metal stirrups locked into place on the table.

"Who delivers the babies way out here?" I asked him.

"If we have time we get them into town; there's a small hospital. If we don't, Leona delivers. She's a trained midwife."

He showed me the nursery next. There were two babies in cribs lying on their stomachs. Their tiny black heads were slick as newborn kittens. They were too young yet to be quite human, almost too fragile to touch. They looked like lonely and mysterious voyagers, exhausted from a long journey. A teenage nurse hovered over them. "The girls all want to come and hold the babies, but Leona doesn't allow it," Henry said. "We send them home as soon as they are able to travel, and we try to get the babies into homes right away, too. It's better that way."

Our next stop was a house trailer that stood on an embankment above the Río Lindo. It was the only place there that had what might be called a vista, down to the riverbed, up to the church. A couple of plastic lounge chairs sat beneath a blue awning. "That's where we live," Henry said. We stood beside the trailer and looked at the garden, a very orderly garden, beans and squash planted between the rows of corn, no weeds.

"Leona takes care of the garden too."

I know, I was about to respond, she's a trained horticulturist, but I didn't get the chance because the paragon herself appeared striding across the grounds with a pile of sheets in her arms. She looked like a woman who wouldn't walk around empty-handed if she could help it. She was about the same age as Henry, fortyish, I guessed, but she was fighting it hard. Behind the sheets she was wearing a shift printed with large flowers. It was sleeveless and came to just above her knees. La Rubia. Her fine blond hair was her best feature, possibly her only feature. The most you could say about her nose was that it was cute. Her eyes and mouth had been painted on, and their expression was perky. Her hair was bouffant, teased underneath and brushed smooth on top. It was the kind of hairdo women wore in the sixties and sprayed with sugar water to keep intact. Maybe the sixties dress and grooming were an attempt to keep time and Mexico at bay, but she was trying too hard. Beneath a facade like that, you could rot or turn to stone. No doubt the cleat marks in the road were hers. I bet she ran in a pastel jogging suit, makeup on and hair done. They were an odd match, Leona and Henry, but I could see they'd struck a balance: he was weak where she was strong, she was strong where he was weak.

Henry introduced us. She said she was pleased to meet me, but her eyes, wrapped in blue eye shadow, didn't show it.

"We don't get many visitors here," she said coldly.

"I would have called first," I replied, "but you don't have a phone."

"We get mail."

I remembered the time in San Miguel that I mailed myself a postcard and it took three weeks to get from the mail slot to my box ten feet away. "I didn't have time," I replied.

Her eyes began to scrunch up in their blue shells. It was bad enough I was there, I was in a hurry besides. She handed the sheets to Henry. "Put these away," she said.

He took the sheets and left like an obedient dog, with one last wag of his tail. "Nice to meet you," he said. "Come see us again."

"Thanks," I replied.

Leona straightened up as Henry walked away. Some people react to Mexico by flexing, some by straightening. She had a stiff back.

"Nice place you got here," I said.

It wasn't any minor job she had undertaken, making order out of Mexico—and not just Mexico but the real essence of the place, the fertility that was its joy and doom. If she thought she could shape up this country she probably wasn't going to tolerate any vagueness from me. We'd only just met, but I could see the time had come to declare my intentions.

"Where did you say you were from?" she began.

"I didn't, but I'm from Albuquerque."

"I'm from El Paso." She turned up the corners of her mouth—I wouldn't exactly call it a smile. "Neighbors."

There's a bumper sticker you see a lot of in New Mexico: IF GOD WANTED TEXANS TO SKI, HE WOULD HAVE PUT MOUNTAINS IN TEXAS. I didn't believe it; Texans made mountains wherever they were.

"What do you do in Albuquerque?"

"I'm a lawyer."

That did it. Her eyes curled up tight. Lawyers have a way of bringing down the lids. "I have a client who adopted a child in Juárez through Licenciado Menendez-Jimenez. I believe you knew him?"

She nodded stiffly, like a doll whose rubber-band joints are too tight.

"I went to see him," I said. "He wasn't able to give me any information before the, um, murder."

If she had any feelings about that matter, she wasn't going to reveal them to me.

"So I traced the adoption records and found the baby was born here."

"Those records are sealed."

"That doesn't mean much in Mexico."

I am not a Mexican and I've got nothing but contempt for

95

the system, her expression said, and that attitude couldn't have made her life in this country a pleasure. "What is it you want here?"

"I want to know who the mother of my client's child is."

She laughed. "Really. And you say you're an attorney? You can't be serious."

"I didn't think it would be easy."

"I can't be bought," she snapped.

"I didn't think you could, but I could still use your help. This *is* something of a special case."

"Every adoption we handle is a special case. The confidentiality of the mother's identity is sacred to us, as is the identity of adoptive parents. That is the bottom line here, for the benefit of all concerned."

"I understand. It's just that my client in Albuquerque, Carl Roberts, has suddenly come before the public eye. He is running for Congress and—"

"Your client is Carl Roberts?" She looked like a clock that had stopped ticking, like someone had just pulled the plug.

"You know him?"

"No." She started ticking again. I didn't suppose her conscience would let her lie, but she sure wasn't telling the whole truth.

"Someone, possibly the mother of Carl's adopted child, has been making threats suggesting that he stole the baby."

"That child wasn't stolen. It was adopted with the mother's full consent."

"It would still be terrible for Carl, terrible for the child if the mother were to appear."

"She won't. The mother doesn't know who has her child. We didn't tell Menendez-Jimenez who the mother was, he didn't tell us who adopted the child. It's our system; no one has all the information."

"Maybe not, but someone could easily put it together if they had the dates, the mothers' names."

"Not here they couldn't. Whoever is bothering your client,

96

it's not the mother." Spun sugar and gloss on the surface, she was beginning to feel like heavy metal underneath. A mixture of anger and disbelief appeared on her face. It wasn't anything I'd said, as she wasn't even looking at me. Her eyes were focused over my shoulder, toward the river. "What the ...?" she began, but before I had a chance to turn around to see what it was that distracted her, I felt my feet leave the ground. I was picked up and spun like a child through the air. The bottom fell out of my stomach. Just as I was about to come down on the ground again, hard, the arms that had lifted and caught me lowered me gently down. It was an attack and an embrace at the same time.

I opened my eyes to find myself lying in the dust and a man leaning over me laughing. Sam. "Hi, Nellie," he said, smiling. "How you been?"

"Just great," I said. "You've got a weird idea of what's fun." Our third meeting. They say once is chance, twice coincidence, three times an enemy action. If Sam wasn't the enemy, it was beginning to look like he must be working for him.

"I didn't hurt you did I?" he said helping me up and brushing me off in places where there wasn't any dust.

"I wouldn't exactly say I enjoy being snuck up on and attacked from behind," I replied, moving away from his brushing hands.

"Sorry about that. Just a little trick I learned in Vietnam. I'm a black belt in karate, did you know that?"

"I do now."

"You were standing there so serious like, I knew you hadn't heard me coming. I thought it would be fun to surprise you." He grinned.

"You two know each other?" Leona asked, as incredulous and angry as her self-control would allow, which was just angry enough to make her spun sugar hairdo quiver.

"We've met," I said.

"What a coincidence," Leona remarked snidely. "How did

you get here anyway?" she asked Sam.

"Just crept up along the riverbank and came around behind the trailer. You could use some water in that river."

"It's always like that at this time of year. You know that," she snapped.

"Pleasure to see you, too, Leona."

"What do you want, Sam?"

"I happened to be in the neighborhood. Thought I'd stop by to say hello."

"You've said it. Now you can get out."

"Hey, Lee, you and I go back a long time, remember."

"The girls were off limits, Sam, you knew that from the very beginning."

"I fell in love. What can I say? I wasn't the only person to ever fall in love here, either."

"Love." She sniffed.

"You're all heart," Sam said, "you know that? I know some girls now in trouble; they need you, you need them. I can put you together, just like the old days."

"No. You and Los Niños are through. Now I suggest you get out of here before you fall in love again."

"Now, Lee."

"Get out. I'm warning you."

"Okay, okay," Sam said. "I can take a hint."

"Why don't you give your friend here a ride when you go. I believe we've said all we have to say, too, but in case there's been a misunderstanding, I'll repeat it. We do not reveal information about our adoptions to anybody. Ever."

"Swell lady," Sam said as we walked down the driveway past the white mushroom chapel.

"She's tough," I said.

It was more than toughness, it was conviction, an absolute conviction that she was right. I'd seen it before. It had to do with religion, a certain kind of Protestant fanaticism. Catholicism was more tolerant. We had reached Sam's

98

vehicle, the red Mazda pickup with racing stripes on the side and New Mexico plates. We got in, he put it in gear and gunned it down the long, dusty road, careening off ruts, obliterating any footprints. He drove as well as a Mexican and was proud of it. The time had come to find out why he kept turning up in my life, so I asked him.

"Just lucky, I guess," was his reply. "We've been traveling in the same circles." He tapped his forehead, revealing the Satan's Sinners tattoo on his forearm and smiling with snaggle-toothed charm. He was charming, all right, friendly as a pup, cute as a scorpion, a combination some women can't resist. I was glad I wasn't one of them.

"I suppose this was the church you were involved with, the one that got you off drugs," I said.

"That's the one. We lived right here in the dorm and in tents and trailers, and the U.S. Government paid for it. Most of us was on Vietnam disability. It was a good place to get off drugs, way out here. Henry was a real fireball in those days, saving people left and right. You see him?"

I nodded.

"He's a wreck of himself; started drinking. Maybe it was us, maybe it was Leona. She could do it to a man. You know, she was a real sweet lady when they moved down here, but the drunker Henry got, the tougher she became. When they got us cured, Leona wasn't ready to quit. They got involved with some rich guy up north and started taking in the girls. Some of those girls have been saved so well, they been back here four or five times." Sam grinned and raised his eyebrows in a Jack Nicholson leer. We had reached the end of Callejón Río Lindo and turned onto the highway.

"What do *you* know about Menendez-Jimenez?" I asked.

"I know he was murdered just when him and me was getting down to talking business. Leona ain't the only one who knows girls in trouble. I don't know for sure who did it, but I got some ideas."

"Anybody I know?"

"Who do I know that you know except me and Leona, and it wasn't me."

I could see that line of questioning was leading nowhere, so I started another.

"What do the girls get for giving up their babies?"

"Help for their families, some money to get started again, things like that."

A hobbled burro stumbled onto the road and stared at us with sad brown eyes. They hobble the burros here to keep them from wandering off, but it doesn't help their odds any on the open highway. While Sam swung out to avoid him, I did some figuring. Say there were fifteen girls at Río Lindo, all of them close to giving birth. Fifteen girls a month at twenty thousand dollars a baby; that was a lot of money. Some cottage cheese and peaches, some palms to be greased, Licenciado Menendez; it still left a nice profit.

"Who is behind this place anyway?" I asked.

"A very rich man, a gringo. I can't tell you his name."

"Why not?"

"He wouldn't like it."

"He's the one who fell in love too?"

"I can't tell you that neither."

"Don't be an asshole, Sam. I didn't come all the way down here because I wanted to visit with Leona. There's a reason why I need to know."

"You tell me what that is, I might tell you his name."

"I can't. It's a matter of client confidentiality."

"Well then I can't tell you who owns this place, Nellie, but a smart lady like you could probably figure it out."

There were a lot of rich gringos out there with interests in Mexico, not so many that I knew, and even fewer who called me Nellie. What was that one doing—sending me out to gather information and following me to make sure I did it? Were there subtle sneaky depths to Carl that even I hadn't discovered yet? "There's a place where I got that name Nel-

100

lie, you know, and it wasn't the cab of a Mazda pickup."

"Any place you want, I'll call you Nellie there too."

"What I want is to know where *you* got that name, why you keep turning up in my life, and who is paying you to do it."

"If someone was paying me, I couldn't tell you anyway, because they'd be my client, right? Client confidentiality."

"Give me a break."

"You think your clients are more important than mine?"

"It better not be the same client."

"Nobody has to pay me, Nellie; I'd do it all by myself," he said with a ragged grin, and then he lit up suddenly like he'd had a brilliant idea. "Are you lookin' for a baby? Is that what you're doin' here? Because if you want to adopt a baby I can get you one, cutest thing you ever saw, and it won't cost you no twenty thousand, neither."

"Jesus Christ," I said.

"Whatsa matter?" he asked. "I say something wrong?"

"It's just you, Sam—you're wrong. Babies aren't something you buy and sell like toothpaste."

"You want it, someone else don't, I can put you together. What's wrong with that?"

"Forget it," I said. "I don't want a baby."

"You'd make a good mother, Nellie."

"Not that good."

If anything I'd said offended him, it didn't show. By the time we reached San Miguel he was telling me about his trip back to Juárez, where Maria was waiting for him, and offering me a ride. I told him I had a round trip ticket on Three Gold Stars. I figured my odds were better on the bus. The drivers drove about as well as Sam, but I'd rather have a bus around me than a Mazda pickup, and it didn't look like I was going to get any more information out of him unless I gave him some, and I wouldn't do that. Besides, it was Semana Santa, Easter week, the most celebrated of all of Mexico's holidays. Maybe I'd find something to celebrate here.

He dropped me several blocks from the hotel; a crowd was already waiting for the Holy Saturday procession and the only way to get through it was to squeeze.

"Nice seein' you again," he said.

"Next time you might give me some warning."

"If I got it to give you I will."

13

A PARADE IS one place where it's an advantage to be a gringa in Mexico—you can see over everyone. You knew they were serious about it because the town had been draped in purple: purple banners hung from the streetlights, purple bunting was draped from the roofs; a dark, *muerto* purple. Street vendors were selling jicama and corn on the cob sprinkled with red chile to eat and papier-mâché replicas of devils and beasts to blow up. I bought one for five hundred pesos for luck, a strange pink beastie about a foot tall with a bird's head and a man's body, fingered hands and webbed feet, and tufts of feathers sticking from its head. It wasn't wired, but most of the demons were sold with explosives tied to their backs. On Easter Sunday Mexico celebrates the ascension into heaven by blowing things up. They like things that go bang in the morning or night, but Saturday is the day of sorrows, the Spanish day. Supposedly in some remote mountain villages, the Crucifixion is actually reenacted, crosses are lashed to men's backs and they carry them through the streets, others flagellate themselves with whips in the square. But in San Miguel they carry the saints from the San Francisco Church to the Paroquia. It's another form of penance, as the saints are heavy life-size wooden statues and it takes eight men to support one on a litter.

I found myself a spot in front of the hotel, leaned against the wall, and waited. The crowd was very subdued, no mariachi bands serenaded under the portal, no newsboys cried, "News," no vendors yelled, *"brocoli, espárragos."* Even the sky had turned gray. The clouds seemed to draw the colors out of the town; the walls lost their terra-cotta pink glow. It was a scene of neutrals, purple and black.

The first sound of the approaching parade was a slow, thin drum and marching feet, then a high-pitched flute. A little child led them, a flutist no more than ten years old. He was dressed in white, intent on the playing of his flute and on each small step. He was followed by three young drummers and then rows of young ladies in white stockings and shoes and confectionery confirmation dresses. "They are all children in Mexico," Peter Esterbrook had said, but there were people here who were older than Peter Esterbrook would ever be. Old ladies with beautiful and wise faces marched along with middle-aged matrons. All the ladies wore black dresses with black lace mantillas and carried prayer books. They were the moral backbone of San Miguel, and their carriage showed it. Next came the wooden saints, the royalty of the parade, bobbing regally above the men who bore the litters. The men's heads were bent; they marched slowly with the patient step and sad eyes of burros. A lot of nights of pulque-induced meanness had to be atoned for. Carved and painted with loving care, the saints were decorated with lace and gilt. They had beautiful complexions and serene expressions. The Virgin, Queen of Sorrows, was last, following a bloodstained effigy of her dying son. She wore a blue wooden robe and her suffering was her ornament and her pride, one pear-shaped tear forever embellishing her cheek. After she was carried up the stairs of the Paroquia and disappeared within, the crowds dispersed. Those there was room for squeezed into the church. The rest slipped silently down the cobblestone streets and back into the *callejóns* and *callecitas* from which they had come.

No one is as sad as a Mexican; no one is as happy, either. On Sunday they celebrated by blowing up a gringo in the *jardín*. It was hard to find a live one to submit to wiring with explosives, so they used a papier-mâché replica. A town as beautiful as San Miguel sees a lot of gringos; gringos dressed in Guatemalan *huipiles, huaraches* with tire soles, the clothes of the poorest of the poor; gringas with peaches-and-cream complexions hardening like crustaceans in the sun. They see old gringos on Social Security, young ones on tour; they see northern European girls in short shorts, no bras, blond hair flying. It's their prerogative to strip naked in the sun, the Mexicans to misinterpret the gesture. After a while in this country, a sane woman learns to cover up, to hide anything that might attract attention.

On Sunday I was awakened early by the sound of a Roman candle whizzing by my window and landing with a thud on a neighboring roof. Cherry bombs were bursting in the street. Mexicans love a parade; they love an explosion even better. By the time I had packed up and eaten one last *bolio* in the hotel's patio, the jardín was filled with the same mourners who had been there yesterday, only today they were in a celebrating mood. The sun came out, and with it the colors. Three mariachi bands competed for space under the portal. Vendors sold *chicharones* and Chiclets. A little boy caught my arm, his eyes bright as diamonds, his face dirty as the mine they came from.

"*Mira, señorita,*" he said. He reached out his hand and plucked a fly from the air. "*Mira, mira,*" he cried happily, palming the fly, then stuffing it into a little object he carried in his hand. He balanced it on his palm for me to see. The minute object, no bigger than a fingernail, was a wooden pig, and as the fly struggled and flapped its wings to escape, it made the pig's ears wiggle and its tail move.

"Only nine hundred pesos," the boy said, his bright eyes turning narrow and crafty in preparation for the deal.

"Too much," I said.

"For you, señorita, eight fifty." His English was perfect when it came to money.

"Too little," I replied. The kid needed the money, the pig needed the fly, the fly needed out of there. Me, too.

I plunged into the *jardín*. People were everywhere—men in plastic sombreros; rebozo-wrapped women with babies; children curled up in the branches of the trees and scooting between the legs of the crowd. They are all children in Mexico, but not for long. The kid with the pig had already left childhood far behind.

The crowd pressed toward the far side of the *jardín* and I let myself get carried with them. Wires were strung from the flat topiary trees to the pink adobe police station across the street, where they sold the sweaters the prisoners knit. Papier-mâché figures dangled from the wires, the smaller ones, green demons about a foot high with curved tails and horned feet and red devils with yellow eyes and insane expressions, on the outside. As the wires got closer to the center of the street, the figures got larger. There were birds and beasts, strange combinations of the human and animal kingdom, spacemen in tinfoil suits, a bare-chested, machine-gun-toting Rambo, and one purple-caped dandy that looked suspiciously like Prince. I saw a couple of four-foot Federales and policemen, but the piâèce de râésistance, bobbing suspended in the center of the street like a fat cork, the one demon that had to be exorcised, was a life-size balding fellow wearing sunglasses and carrying a copy of *Time* magazine in his back pocket, his camera dangling from his neck and balancing on his fat belly—the Gringo.

I glanced quickly around. There weren't many live gringos visible, scared off by the impending catharsis. As every attorney knows, there are times when it's advantageous to be conspicuous, maybe even to be a pain in the ass, but this wasn't one of them. I've always believed that if you don't put out troublesome vibes, you won't be troubled. As I was congratulating myself for being only a token gringa, for not even owning a camera, there was a sudden hush. I looked around furtively, just to make sure it had nothing to do with me.

Drums rolled, and then, *kaboom!* a green demon exploded, shooting a thousand green bullets through the air.

106

With squeals of delight, children laughed and scrambled to pick up the pieces. Another window-rattling blast and a red devil burst. *Bang!* a mad dog; *bam!* a bull. Each demise was accompanied by squeals of merriment, another irritant exorcised, but it was just foreplay. The main moment, the one they'd all gathered here to see was the disintegration of Mr. G. After enough explosives had been detonated to change the fortunes of a small country and the *jardín* smelled like the field of battle, he was the only devil left.

The climactic moment was extended by a fuse that wouldn't stay lit. Drums rolled while someone, in a mixture of stupidity and bravado, climbed way out on the swaying limb of a topiary tree and rewired him. As I waited, getting mentally smaller and darker, too embedded in the crowd to leave, too perverse to want to, I noticed moving among the black heads across the street one spun sugar blond.

La Rubia, not one to adopt protective coloring in a crowd. Her face was as immaculately painted and fixed in expression as a wooden saint's. She moved with calm authority, ignoring the Gringo overhead, the merriment at her side. As I had expected, she carried a plastic shopping bag, which seemed to be empty. She was intent on something. I didn't think it was canned peaches for the evening meal.

I wanted to know what it was, and I was starting to push my way through the crowd to follow her when Mr. G finally blew in a tremendous explosion that sent whatever birds still remained in San Miguel fleeing—possibly forever—that must have startled even the girls in Río Lindo; that made me jump, although I had sworn I wouldn't. The shock of the event and my neighbors' glee over it rooted me to my place, but Leona kept right on going, disappearing around the corner and never even bothering to turn her head.

14

———

IT WAS A long trip back by bus and taxi, airplane and car, and it was hard to believe it was the same day—Easter Sunday—when I got home. I argued with the taxi driver in Mexico City over the tip and with the parking lot attendant in Albuquerque about the price of bailing out the Rabbit. "I thought this was the economy lot," I said. "You want your car back?" he replied. In Mexico City I had filled the cabdriver's hand with pesos, but it wasn't enough. His hand changed from a dirty palm with fingers to a deep well while I dropped in the coins.

"Bastante," I said finally.

"But you have so much money, señorita," he said, his hand reaching out for more.

"Not that much," I replied.

I had a lot of time to think en route, and I didn't like where my thoughts were leading. They went from Leona to Sam to Carl to a very rich man.

In my absence spring had arrived in the Duke City. As we made our approach to Albuquerque International, I could see the unmistakable signs of the season—a cloud of dust that buried all the old familiar landmarks: McDonald's, Baja Tacos, Dairy Queen. Spring in New Mexico means wind—not breezes, *wind*. Wind that smashes tumbleweeds into your car and dust into your eyes, that whips your hair around, that howls and tears at the windows until it unsettles your brain.

It was still Easter Sunday. Maybe when I got home I would find a basket with green cellophane grass, yellow duckies, and chocolate bunnies on my doorknob. It wasn't there, but

I found a bottle of Cuervo Gold in the cupboard and a Lean Cuisine in the fridge. I preheated the oven to four hundred, put some ice in a glass, poured the Cuervo Gold over the ice, opened the freezer, took out the frozen dinner, read the instructions. "Preheat oven to 400°," it said (I'd already done that), "take dinner out of box, take off paper cover, insert dinner in oven." While it cooked, I turned on KUNM. *The Singing Wire* was playing Indian chants that were a whole lot sweeter than the sound of the wind. I woke up to find someone pounding on the door and smoke pouring from the oven. It was three A.M. The Kid was at the door.

"Your house is burning, chiquita," he said.

"That's what happens when you don't cook very often—you lose your touch," I told him, opening the oven door. Zucchini lasagna; charred pasta in a tin dish.

The Kid didn't know or care that it was Easter. As a matter of fact, it wasn't Easter anymore; it was the day after.

"Why do you always show up at three in the morning?" It was the smoke that made my eyes water, but that pathetic whining voice sounded just like Judy Bates, a victim let out of the bag.

"I'm sorry, chiquita. I play music tonight."

"You always come here *after* you play music."

"You care about that?"

Did I? Did I want it any different? How different?

The Kid put his arm around me. "I'm sorry, chiquita. I come early some night if you want. I come for dinner." He looked at the charred lasagna and grinned. I didn't. "Manny tells me you come to the shop."

"I happened to be in the neighborhood."

"Why you not come to the house? I played music that night, but my cousin was there. She'd be glad to see you."

"Your cousin?"

"Sure." He laughed. I smiled. I threw the Lean Cuisine away.

But later I thought, his cousin, what does that mean? He

109

was still awake, sort of. "That 'cousin' of yours," I asked, "is she pretty?"

He shrugged. "She's just a girl. She doesn't even speak English."

In the morning I let my pink demon out of the suitcase and showed it to him, as the Kid was finding it hard to believe that I had been to Mexico. He wasn't much interested in picturesque mountain towns or fiestas, either. He shrugged when I mentioned San Miguel. "Sure I been there. How much you pay for that?" He poked the web-footed demon.

"Five hundred pesos."

"Five hundred pesos?" He shook his head.

"It's folk art," I said. "I like him. Why are you so negative about your country? What's wrong with parades and fiestas?"

He looked at me like I'd gone round the bend. "It's superstition," he said. "Why did you go down there?"

"On business. I went for a client who has interests in Mexico."

"In Mexico." The idea that anyone would go to Mexico on business was incredible to him. The U.S. was where you went on business; you didn't go to Mexico at all if you could help it.

"Listen, Kid, there's something I've been meaning to ask you. Do you know what *el perro dogo* means?"

"Sure, it's a kind of a dog, short but big like a bull. When he take you in his mouth like this he don't let go."

When I got to the office at midday, spring had preceded me to Hamel and Harrison. The door was wide open and Anna and Brink were sitting in the reception room staring into space. It looked like they'd fallen in love, but not with each other, thank God. A big vase of lilacs on Anna's desk had an essence-of-springtime smell.

"The lilacs are out," I said.

"They sure are," said Brink with a moony expression. "I picked some for Sally, too."

110

"Sally?"

"I went there for Easter dinner yesterday. She cooked a leg of lamb. Can you believe it? A leg of lamb for the two of us. What a woman." He shook his head in sated disbelief.

"A leg of lamb," I said. "And you didn't suspect anything?"

"What do you mean?" asked Brink suspiciously, wondering if I'd be enough of a shit to say something that would ruin his day.

I might. "And you let her get away with it."

"With what?"

"The evidence. Didn't you ever see the Alfred Hitchcock show where a woman kills her husband with a frozen leg of lamb and then cooks it and feeds it to the police so there'll be no evidence?"

"Ha, ha," said Brink.

"Did *you* have a nice Easter?" asked Anna. So someone was going to ask about me.

"Lovely," I said. "I went to Mexico."

"Mexico?" she asked. I gave her a warning, straight-arm look. "Mexico. Oh, that's right, I just forgot for a minute. How was Mexico?"

"Interesting," I said.

I figured Brink *had* fallen in love; he didn't even mention Carl Roberts, and Carl Roberts and Mexico were linked in his mind like Stalin and Russia, the Ayatollah Khomeini and Iran, Nixon and the U.S.A.

In a generous mood, having already forgiven Anna for forgetting that I went to Mexico, I asked her about her Easter.

"Fantastic," she said.

She spent it with Yellow Mustache, who by now had a name—George—and an occupation—computer salesman. Anna had her George; Brink, his Sally; Neil was reunited with her Kid. What a trio of mismatched couples—but wasn't that what romance was all about? I was ready to sit on the doorstep and moon with them. There was a rich man out there somewhere needing to be located, but it didn't have to be right now.

But it did, because the phone rang and it was Peter Esterbrook on the line. I didn't know anybody richer than him.

"I'd like to talk to you Miss Hamel," he said. "Could you come by the farm this afternoon around four?"

"I could, but I think the person you want to speak to is Carl. Come to mention it, I'd like to speak to him too."

"No, it's you I want to speak to. I'd appreciate it if you would be here."

I went. It was Carl's problem, and I shouldn't have gone, but I did.

15

THE LILACS HAD come into bloom at Esterbrook Farms, too, a mass of lavender and white. Wind is the bitter part of spring in New Mexico, lilacs are the sweet. Already sprinklers were sprinkling the lawn, nourishing green shoots. Already the gardeners were out supervising the sprinklers, tending the plants. Peter stood waiting for me on the portal, wearing a white shirt, blue jeans with creases in them, and a belt with a silver and turquoise buckle. He looked tall, healthy, tan, southwestern. He smiled, showing perfect white teeth, while his eyes studied me coldly. The pots of pink geraniums on the portal and the hand carved door framed him well, like a page from *Town and Country*.

"Lovely day," he remarked. Of course it was, but getting less so. Even the wind didn't intrude at Esterbrook Farms. The mass of lilacs kept it from disturbing Peter's peace, but if an occasional gust did get through the bushes, there was little to ruffle, few loose edges. Every surface at Esterbrook Farms was planted and manicured. No wild chamisa or purple sage snuck in here. The grass kept the earth in place, the walk was closely fitted brick, the driveway graveled, the flower beds tended. The only disorderly elements were the beat-up Volkswagen in the driveway and the gardeners; three Mexicans who played Mexican music on their radio while they worked and an Anglo with a long blond ponytail who was potting some geraniums at the other end of the portal.

"I see you hire Anglos, too," I said as Peter led me into the house.

"I hire people who get the work done. Kiefer happens to be a thorough and sometimes even inspired worker. Very determined to get the job, too, I might add. He thought Esterbrook Farms would be a good showcase for his gardening skills, and he came to me looking for work. I haven't been disappointed, although I don't much care for the way he looks. Unfortunately there was a time when all the young people in New Mexico looked like that."

"They're not so young anymore now that that time has come and gone."

"It couldn't have gone soon enough to suit me. But I will say that in spite of his appearance, Kiefer has proven to be a very satisfactory employee."

"I talked to him at your party about the wild irises on Hamilton Mesa."

"Yes, well, Kiefer is enamored of Mother Nature."

"I suppose the Volkswagen belongs to him."

"Yes."

We walked down the hallway past the living room where Don Quixote stood at parade arrest. I could see the patio, caught in a beam of sunshine. As we walked toward it, I heard the fountain tinkling and a parrot squawk. I also heard the delicate sound of children's voices, chirping like birds.

"Carl is out of town. Celina went shopping and I have the children for the day," Peter said.

We entered the patio; the decor was Mexican, I couldn't yet speak for its soul. The children were playing on the tile floor with a toy, a little mechanical dragon that shot fire sparks from its mouth and tottered on the bricks. They laughed as it fell over.

"Have you met the children?" Peter asked, "Emma and Edward."

The children looked up. "Yes," I replied, "at the party."

"Hello," they said. Even Emma looked animated today, her blond curls tousled, a flush of excitement in her cheeks. And Eduardo—he, too, had that Esterbrook air of being al-

114

most too perfect, and I thought again how odd but in a way how right that this child had ended up in this family. They were opposite in type, but alike in beauty. Eduardo, however, was distinguished by his eyes. They didn't have the sort of ingenuousness that you found in Celina's, the coldness of Peter's. Eduardo's eyes were old and sad and patient and wise.

Geraniums were blooming in terra-cotta pots shaped like goats and deer. A bougainvillea was growing up the south-facing wall. The chairs were those straight-backed, tippy leather ones from Mexico that are nice to look at but bondage to sit in.

"Lupe," Peter called, raising his voice just a notch, but his voice was so controlled, up a notch was as effective as a shout.

Lupe, the Mexican maid, entered quickly and silently from a doorway that led to one of the wings of the house. She was wearing a white uniform. Except that she didn't appear to be pregnant, she might have been one of the girls at Río Lindo. She was dark, with almond-shaped, serious eyes; her hair was pulled back and tied at the nape of her neck. She had flat Indian cheekbones and a wary air. She and Eduardo were cut from the same dignified Mexican cloth.

"Come, children," she said. "It's time to feed the animals." Eduardo turned immediately, and they seemed for an instant as the sun played across the patio to be connected by fine, shimmery webbing.

"I always have them feed the dogs and horses when they visit," Peter told me. "It's good for them, gives them a sense of responsibility. The horses take the carrots right out of their hands. The children don't touch the dogs, of course; my dogs are guard dogs, not pets. But I let them pour the food into the pens."

"Come, Emma," Lupe said quietly.

"No," Emma replied.

"Come," Lupe repeated.

115

"I don't want to." Emma pouted, sticking out her lower lip.

"Yes, you do, young lady," Peter said raising his voice another notch, the Obey notch. "You want to go right now."

Emma looked at him defiantly but she went, already aware, no doubt, of doting Grandpa's prickly side.

"Lupe seems to be good with the children," I said.

"She came to me late last year, well recommended by an associate of mine; I haven't been disappointed. Perhaps you'd care for some iced tea," Peter suggested, his voice dropping down again to Host. A pitcher stood on the leather table, amber-colored in the sun, with slices of lemon floating on top.

"Thank you," I replied. He poured me a glass and suggested we take it to his study at the other end of the house. I followed him across the courtyard. If the living room was suitable for a Spanish grandee, the study belonged to an English country squire. There was a large fireplace with a mantel, an Oriental rug on the floor, worn leather furniture, and bookcases from floor to ceiling. The only place I'd seen so many books in recent years was the law library at Lovell Cruse. French doors stood open to the balmy spring day and the smell of lilacs, a terrace and the lawn beyond. Across the lawn I could see part of the barn and next to it a bunch of dog pens. Inside their chain link pens the dogs, Dobermans mostly, lazed or slept. Actually, the one thing missing from the room itself was a dog, a floppy kind of spaniel lying on the floor, and I told Peter I thought he should bring one inside.

"I don't keep animals for amusement," Peter said. "My dogs work for me, and they are trained for one purpose only—protection. That's what they excel at, that's what they do. If they have reason to believe they are threatened, they attack. They patrol the property at night and when I am not here. No one enters this property without my consent."

Nevertheless, it would have been nice to have some old

116

Spot to curl up at my feet while I waited for Peter to begin his pitch. He sat down at an antique desk that wasn't much bigger than mine, but a whole lot neater. The only things he had out were a green blotter and a silver letter opener. I sat down in front of him.

"We might as well get right to the point here, Miss Hamel," he began.

"You may call me Neil," I replied.

He picked up the letter opener, apparently no longer inclined to call me anything at all. "It may or may not surprise you to know that I am the owner of Los Niños de los Angeles."

I recrossed my legs and wished I had a dog's head to fondle, some ears to scratch. I didn't say anything; what could I say? If it did surprise me, I was stupid. If it didn't, paranoid.

"Leona called and told me you had been there," Peter said.

I laughed. That was where she was hustling off to on Sunday—*el teléfono*. "*That* doesn't surprise me," I said.

"What do you mean?"

"Nothing. She seemed like a very efficient woman."

"She does her job. She wouldn't be working for me if she didn't. I consider myself an excellent judge of character; I don't hire people who don't perform." And who else did he hire to perform? I wondered, but it didn't seem like the right moment to ask. He tapped at the blotter with the letter opener. I could see the initials engraved on the handle, P.G.E.

"The news she gave me was most disturbing, as you can imagine. You told her my son-in-law has been receiving threats having to do with the adoption of Edward."

"With Carl's permission, I told her."

"What does that mean?"

"I am Carl's attorney. I can discuss this case with his permission only. I was authorized to speak to Leona. I haven't been authorized to speak to you."

"That's ridiculous. Carl is my son-in-law."

"Then you should talk to him."

"He's out of town, and this is a matter of immediate and grave concern to me. I want you to tell me what took place."

"I can't."

His voice was like air conditioning, a running motor that kept the elements outside the window, but it was breaking down and the hot air was sneaking in. "Your obstinacy is most annoying," he said. "Edward's welfare is my concern. I have a right to know."

And I had the right to remain silent. "I am sorry," I said, "but I do not reveal a client's confidences. Ever." Leona couldn't have done it better.

Peter Esterbrook was not accustomed to being refused. He studied me across his desk as if it were an open field and I was a distant prey. I watched the view through the French doors. Lupe and the children were crossing the lawn. She carried the dogs' food and some carrots for the horses in a basket in one hand and held on to Emma with the other. Eduardo ran ahead of them. He was playing with a red balloon that he tossed into the air and tried to catch with wide open arms. When it fell to the ground he kicked it, then tossed it up again.

Peter tapped at the blotter with the letter opener. "I must say I'm most curious to know why my son-in-law sent you to Mexico."

"I am his attorney."

"You? There are a number of competent attorneys in Carl's firm," he said with what might be seen as over-emphasis on *competent*.

"Carl didn't want to involve his firm."

"He could have come to me."

"But he didn't, did he? *I'd* like to know how you could arrange an adoption for Carl without him knowing."

"I didn't arrange it; a lawyer in Juárez did, as I am sure you are aware."

118

"You own Los Niños de los Angeles."

"Carl doesn't know that."

"Why not? He's your son-in-law."

"It's my nature. I am a private man. I don't discuss my affairs with anyone, including my family."

I assumed that also meant his daughter, who, as it happened, had just come around the corner of the house. I watched through the French doors as Celina walked alone across the lawn toward Lupe and the children, pale and elegant as always in a pink dress and high-heeled sandals. She stopped to take off her sandals and continued barefoot across the lawn.

"You might favor me with your attention, Miss Hamel."

"So your daughter and son-in-law adopted a baby from an agency you own, and you're telling me you had nothing to do with it."

"I won't deny that I tried to find them the most suitable baby, but that's all."

"Then you know who the mother is."

"I don't see what that has to do with anything."

"You don't? When Carl is receiving threats from someone, possibly the mother?"

"I thought you were a bright woman. Only a fool would believe the mother was responsible."

"Well, if you know who is responsible then why are you bothering me?"

"It's perfectly obvious to me that it's one of Carl's political opponents, and I intend to find out which one."

"Right." My gaze had strayed to the open window again. I couldn't see Celina's face from where I sat, but I imagined she was smiling at the children. Suddenly she stopped and put her hand to her mouth as if to smother a scream. I followed her stare across the lawn, through the spray of sprinklers that were watering it. Emma and Lupe were at the far side of the lawn beside the chain link fence that caged the dogs. Lupe had dropped her basket and the carrots

119

spilled onto the ground. She, too, was standing deathly still. The whole scene was like a freeze-frame, children playing the game of statues frozen in place. Lupe gripped Emma's hand. Emma seemed to be crying, but they were far enough away that I couldn't hear. It was a silent, still tableau, seen from a distance that made me powerless to affect it.

The door to one of the dog pens had swung open and Eduardo was standing inside the pen facing one of Peter's well-trained guard dogs. The dog stood as tall as Eduardo. He was big and powerful and mean. His ears were pinned back and his fangs were bared. I couldn't hear it, but I knew there was a vicious growl in his throat. He was an attack dog ready to attack, and I saw why—Eduardo had startled him and violated his space. The red balloon lay on the ground between them.

"Oh, my God," I said.

"What is it?" Peter leapt up, the silver letter opener still in his hand. He ran from behind his desk to the French doors and then stopped himself. I knew why. Dogs perceive motion, not substance. How could the dog know it was his master, Peter Esterbrook, at this distance? It would be just a glimmer of movement to startle and threaten him. Eduardo stood absolutely still, a totally unnatural posture for a little boy. It was an eternal moment; the fragile child, the dog that snarled in nasty rage, the rest of us not daring to move. A gust of wind found its insolent way through Peter's lilacs. It danced across the lawn, leapt, whirled, caught the balloon, spun it into the air and dropped it against the dog's chest. He lunged then with all the speed and meanness that had been bred and trained into him, and he had the boy down on the ground just like that.

"Shep, halt, stop it!" Peter yelled, grabbing for a silver whistle he kept on a hook by the door. It made a sound much too high-pitched for humans to hear, but Shep heard it. He let go of Eduardo and looked in confusion at his master, then snarled at the boy. He was only doing what he had been trained to.

Celina screamed, a tense, shrill sound like glass breaking. And then the shot came, the sound of a high-powered rifle. It hit the dog in the shoulder, just inches away from the boy. The dog yipped and fell back. There was the crack of another shot; this one hit Shep's neck and he fell over, dead. As the life went out of him, all the other dogs began to howl. We were all running, but Lupe was the first to reach Eduardo. She picked him up, his blood smearing her white uniform. He grabbed her neck and buried his face against her shoulder. Peter reached them, but he made no move to take the child.

"Is he all right?" he said.

"Mi niño," Lupe mumbled. *"Mi niño."*

The shot had come from the stable doorway. The person who fired it was walking toward us with the rifle in his hand, the barrel pointed down toward the ground. He was a short man with broad shoulders, brown hair clipped close to his head.

It was Andrew Monogal.

16

"ANDERS, I AM SO deeply indebted to you," Peter
Esterbrook said, using the German version of Andrew's
name. His voice was about as warm as the air in the bar
refrigerator he was leaning against. The rest of us sat in the
Prado room on sofas and chairs that were not what I'd call
user friendly. Celina was an empty glass teetering on the
edge of the sofa; one light tap would have made her *ping* deli-
cately, then shatter. We were awaiting word from the doctor
who was examining Eduardo in the boy's room. Eduardo had
his own room in Peter's house and it was Peter who insisted
that he be taken there, not to the hospital, and it was Peter's
doctor who came immediately when called.

Peter was the only one who spoke. The rest of us were
struck dumb by the incident. It seemed that if no one left the
room or talked, everything would come out all right. The
only way Peter knew how to make things right—or wrong—
was to give orders. Carl was on his way back from a campaign
appearance in Silver City. Lupe, still in her blood-stained
uniform, sat on the sofa next to Emma and Celina. Monogal
stood at the bar with Peter, giving no hint that our eyes had
met once across a crowded room. No one questioned what I
was doing there; they were too worried about Eduardo to
notice me. Of them all I had the least reason to be there, and
I wasn't eager to be, but I was trapped, unable to step outside the doorway until this episode was over.

Peter put his hand on Monogal's shoulder, a gesture I
wouldn't exactly call an embrace. Monogal stood at attention and didn't say a word, but I saw a slight smile, subtle as

springtime, move across his jowly face, and just for a second, in spite of the number of cubic feet he occupied, in spite of his bulldog charm, he looked like a sly little boy getting away with something he knew he'd done wrong, a kid who had just killed his pet gerbil and was letting somebody else take the rap.

Something tied these two together; it didn't look like love to me.

"Thank God you are such a superb marksman. Can I ever repay you, Anders?" Peter Esterbrook asked.

"Yes," said Monogal. It was the first time I'd heard him speak, and his voice was deep and reluctant, as if he didn't use it often.

"We'll talk," Peter said.

Monogal, who managed to seem pathetic and mean at the same time, looked as if talk were the last thing on his mind, but whatever was occupying him got put aside, because at that moment the doctor entered the room.

"You'll be happy to know that he will be all right," the doctor said. "He'll be just fine."

Celina began to cry.

"Gracias a Dios," said Lupe.

"Will he be scarred?" asked Peter.

"Not noticeably. His face was practically unmarked; the bites were in the neck and shoulder area and they should heal nicely. He's resting comfortably now."

The beauty would remain intact, then, but you had to wonder about the scars inside. An apparently secure world shattered like that by a gate carelessly—or not so carelessly?—left open, a grandfather's vicious dog.

"Well," said Peter, "this calls for a celebration!" He opened the bar refrigerator, took a bottle of Stolichnaya from the freezer, and poured everyone an ice-cold shot. Celina, who needed something stronger than vodka, stared into her glass.

"Don't sip, drink it down," Peter said.

123

"I can't. It's too strong."

Chugging never bothered me. I can drink vodka just about as fast as I drink tequila. I swallowed my shot and was thinking about asking for another when Celina turned and looked at me like she was waking from a deep sleep. Or maybe she hadn't awakened yet, maybe she was still dreaming. Maybe the dream was a nightmare and she found me in it. "Neil," she said in a dazed voice, "what are you doing here?"

"I had an appointment with your father." If someone was going to lie about my presence, it needn't be me.

"Miss Hamel is advising me on a land purchase," Peter said, smooth and cold as the vodka.

"But Carl does your legal work," said Celina.

"He does," Peter replied, "but there was a conflict of interest in this case, as the firm represents the owner. Would it be all right, Doctor, if Celina and Lupe went in to see Edward now?"

"I gave him some sedation and he's sleeping, but I think it would be fine."

Celina and Lupe left the room together, the adoptive mother and the Mexican maid, united by love for a boy. I wondered exactly how much Celina, or even Peter, knew about Lupe. I'd bet it was a lot less than Lupe knew about them. It's the servant who studies the master, the master who takes the servant for granted.

"It was criminal negligence to leave that gate open," Peter said angrily once the women had left the room. "Now I am going to find out who did it, and I am going to find out why. If you will excuse me, gentlemen. Please help yourselves to another drink."

I wasn't averse to another drink, but I wasn't a gentleman, and having no particular desire to spend any more time in the same room with Andrew Monogal, I said, "I guess I'll be on my way." No one asked me to linger, so I made my exit down the hallway, feet slinking along the slick carpet.

I let myself out the antique door and went down the brick

path, noticing as I did how the lilacs bloomed, lavender and white pom-poms, swaying on bushes as tall as a tree. The lawn was coming along nicely; the sprinklers tickety-ticked, the cottonwoods showed the first hint of green, the geraniums blossomed under the portal. I listened to the driveway gravel crunching beneath my feet crunch by crunch and watched the clouds float across the enormous New Mexico sky, images of forgetfulness and knowing. I got all the way to my car, put my hand on the door handle—but of course in the excitement I had forgotten my purse. Since my keys were inside, I had to go back to get it, and since I was going in anyway, I should go to the bathroom, as it was a long drive home.

I passed the doctor on the path.

"Forgot my purse," I said, and stopped to be polite.

"Beautiful place Peter has here, isn't it?" he asked.

"Oh, it is. But what a frightening thing to have happen."

"Terrible. Children can give you such a scare."

I agreed and elaborated and killed some more time saying good-bye. A good good-bye can stick like flypaper if you let it, but what does time mean anyway measured by cumulonimbus billowing and disintegrating in the wild western sky? I left the doctor and walked around the side of the house, the side I hadn't seen yet. Peter's house was rectangular, four wings with a courtyard in the middle.

This side didn't reveal much more than the rest of the building; a white wall, a lovingly tended lawn, a harmonious arrangement of daffodils and tulips in bloom next to the house. There was a door about halfway down the wall, the kitchen probably; the remnants of an herb garden were next to it. I recognized the stubs of parsley, dead for the winter, about to spring back to life. The dog pens and the barn were behind the house, approachable from either side, but I preferred this one as it was the side away from Peter's study.

The dogs' runs connected with the barn, and someone had let them inside and shut the doors. Shep's body had been disposed of. I could see his pen from where I stood behind the house. Part of the pens and barn were visible from Peter's study, the remainder extended behind the corner of the house. As all the dogs' pens appeared to be the same, I examined the closest one. There was a door in the chain link fencing that opened into each run, so that the dogs could be let in or out individually. There were dishes attached to the inside of the door and a flap for food and water to be poured through. The door to the run I was looking at was latched. I reached through the chain link fence, unlatched the gate, and pushed at the food flap. The door swung open.

Esterbrook Farms would have a door that swung easily, but it only swung in. The dogs couldn't get out if the door were left unlatched, but somebody could get in. It was apparent that the children spent a lot of time here; the dogs must have known them. I wondered what had set Shep off. That his space had been invaded? That he was startled by the red balloon? Or maybe he was just mean and vicious. It took a certain kind of arrogant stupidity to keep attack dogs around children, but it wasn't uncommon, as evidenced by all the people who keep pit bulls. Lawyers could survive and probably prosper just by representing claims against pit bulls. It could have been an accident that the gate was left open; it could have been deliberate. Who knew?

At the end of the pens where I was standing, a door opened into the barn, a long white building with a red roof. As I approached the doorway, I heard men talking, in English and Spanish. In most bilingual places people speak one language at a time; here, if they knew how, they spoke both.

"*Puta madre.* I should have known better than to trust that *chingarra.* He's got too much money. Never trust anybody with mucho money, amigos," Kiefer, the gardener, said. He was throwing work clothes and gardening tools into a duffel bag while the Mexican gardeners watched morosely.

"Excuse me," I said from the doorway. "I didn't mean to

interrupt." Although that's exactly what I had meant to do.

"You're not," Kiefer said, and went right on packing.

"I think I met you at Carl's party. I'm Neil Hamel."

"Kiefer—Kiefer the asshole. You won't be seeing me around this place anymore. I'm outta here right now, taking nothing but the tools I brought with me. That's okay. There's a lot of land in this state that don't belong to Peter Esterbrook. Maybe I'll get some rich old lady in Santa Fe to give me a job. Excuse me if Esterbrook's a friend of yours. He's still a *chingarra.* "

"No friend of mine. I do some legal work for his son-in-law, that's all."

"You a lawyer?" He stopped packing for a minute, took a good look at a rusty spade. "You want this, José? It's yours."

"Ai, no, gracias, " said José.

"Go ahead, take it. You deserve it. You need all the help you can get if you're gonna work here. He's a coldhearted son of a bitch. Here's something for you too, Paco."

"Muchas gracias. " José and Paco looked as if they were going to cry. No one is as sad as a sad Mexican.

"A lawyer, huh. Well, whattaya think about this? Criminal negligence. He says I left the gate open and that's how the kid got into the pen. I was criminally negligent and he intends to prosecute. Do you believe it, after all I done for that guy? This place was the desert when I got here. And for peon wages, too. Excuse me, José, Paco, but it's true. The pay here is shit. Well, I can get by without Peter Esterbrook, and he is going to have to look a long way if he thinks he is going to prosecute me."

"It would be a very hard thing to prove."

"Damn right—and you know why? I didn't do it, that's why."

"Any idea who did?"

"How the fuck would I know? I just work here—or did. I don't no more."

"My number's in the book. Give me a call if you have any

ideas. Maybe I can help. And I wouldn't go too far away if I were you. You've got a real feel for the area. It's the grounds that make this place."

"Yeah, well, thanks." He threw some work gloves into the bag and zipped it up.

I walked back the way I'd come and let myself in through the front door. The house was very quiet. I remembered there was a bathroom down the hallway, from which I'd seen Carl emerge at the party. I walked down the hallway and pulled open a door that let me reluctantly into the dining room and then swung slowly shut behind me. The dining room continued the medieval theme with a gargantuan wooden chandelier and table and chairs to match.

A swinging door let me into the kitchen, the one room where Peter recognized the twentieth century. Everything in the kitchen was the latest in culinary technology: microwaves and Cuisinarts. I saw the door that opened onto the herb garden, and another door, which opened into Lupe's room, right next to the kitchen, naturally. In this room I was a voyeur, and I walked through it quickly and out the other side. I couldn't help but notice how bare and temporary it seemed. There was nothing but a bed, a bureau, a color TV; the walls were painted an institutional green. The only personal touch was a beautiful hand carved wooden cross on the wall.

I was back in the hallway and turned the corner into the children's wing. Undoubtedly there would be a bathroom here. There was also a room done Little Girl, pink and ruffled with dolls on the bed but no little girl inside. Little Boy was right next door. Since I was there anyway, I looked in.

The decor was Latin American, with brilliant fabric animals and trees on the wall. The little boy was in bed, sleeping, his head wrapped in a large white bandage, surrounded by pillows and a teddy bear. Perhaps Celina had taken to her own bed with something stronger than vodka—she probably had a room here somewhere, too—because Eduardo was

128

alone with Lupe, who sat in a chair next to him, a turquoise Mexican chair with a rush seat too close to the floor for a gringa to be able to get into. The blood on her uniform had dried and turned brown. Her hair hung in a braid down her back; her cheekbones were high, dignified, Indian. She was very still, very erect, infinitely patient. She would sit by this bed for a lifetime if that would do Eduardo any good. Mexican servants can seem invisible, they move so quietly around a house, but there are moments when everyone else is sleeping or gone and you wonder who is really in possession of the place. They are the ones who sweep the evil spirits away from the door, who light candles to keep the benevolent ones within.

I paused, perhaps for too long, in the doorway, and Lupe looked up. Her eyes were steady and unsurprised. They said nothing, except that she knew who I was and possibly why I was there and that she could outwait and outserve and out-mystify me any day of the year.

"Is he all right?" I asked.

"*Sí,*" she replied. "*Gracias a Dios.*"

"I was looking for the bathroom."

"*Allá.*" she motioned me down the hallway.

"Thank you," I said.

"It's nothing."

But once that was finished, I still had to get my purse, so I crossed the courtyard to the den. The fountain seemed subdued, as if even the water knew it was time to shut up. Someone had thrown a cover over the parrot's cage. The deer and goat flowerpots stood erect, and their horns and antlers made shadows on the tile floor. The bougainvillea had climbed another fraction of an inch. The carpet swallowed my footsteps as I walked toward Peter the Great's study—there probably was a Russian room in here somewhere, too; the bedroom, maybe, draped in furs. The thick walls muffled the sounds in the study. I could hear voices but not words, only, at the last minute, "I honor my contracts even when they don't turn out to my advantage. I have given my word; those papers will be signed," spoken with icy control.

"Forty years I've been with you and it ends like this."

"If it is so important to you, I will give your money back, and let me say that I consider that a more than generous offer. Now I suggest you let go of it, Anders; it's over. There are other businesses you can run, other things to do in life."

By now I was only one step away from the doorway. I heard the French doors slam and the glass rattle in the frame, I saw the svelte Peter Esterbrook watching the unsvelte Andrew Monogal clomp across the lawn. I waited what seemed like a decent interval to me and knocked at the door. "Beg your pardon," I said.

If looks could do it, his would have turned me into something hard and unpleasant on the spot. "Forgot my purse." And, just to prove I wasn't an eavesdropper or a voyeur, there it was, exactly where I had left it, on the floor in front of Peter's desk. By now I could see Monogal passing the dog pens and heading for the barn. I noticed that Peter had hung his whistle back on the wall.

"Time to feed the dogs?" I said.

"And what is that supposed to mean?"

"Is he one of your loyal employees, too?"

"As a matter of fact, he is," Peter replied slowly, lingering over each word like it was sour candy and he liked the bitter taste. "He runs some of my business ventures. He also manages the animals and property when I'm not here, among other things. And yes, so you won't need to ask, I keep my guns in the barn. Anders had a perfectly good reason to be there. It was very careless—it was more than careless, it was criminal for the gardener to leave that gate open. Shep was a recent addition, here on a trial basis. Quick, but high-strung and nervous, the one dog I wasn't absolutely sure of around the children. Kiefer knew that, and I should know better than to hire hippies, no matter how well they care for my

130

plants. And I have nothing further to say to you, Miss Hamel, not now, and with any good fortune, not ever again."

17

I WAITED UNTIL noon the next day. Since Carl hadn't called me, I called him.

"Hey, Neil," Angie said, "how you doin'? I'll get him."

Carl came on the line. "So glad you called, Neil. That was a terrible thing yesterday, terrible. Very upsetting for Celina. For all of us."

"How's Eduardo?"

"He's still sedated, but the doctor says he'll be all right. Peter fired Kiefer, the gardener."

"So I heard."

"You may not have heard everything. Kiefer, it turns out, was active in the anti-WIPP movement. As a matter of fact he spent some time in jail for protesting at the site."

"So?"

"So I come out in favor of the WIPP project, Kiefer talks Peter into hiring him, I get threatening notes, and someone leaves the door to Shep's run open when they know Edward will be nearby. Peter thinks the anti-WIPP forces are using Edward to intimidate us."

"Why?"

"Well, because they don't want WIPP to go through and I'm the only candidate who's for it."

"And why else, may I ask?"

"Possibly because Peter owns the Mother Lode. Maybe they thought if they got to me they could prevent him from negotiating with the Department of Energy for WIPP, but it's too late now."

"Then why was Menendez-Jimenez murdered?"

"Maybe there was no connection. As you said, I'm not the only client he ever had."

"I said that?"

"Yes, you did."

"And what about the file that was stolen from my office and the fact that I came very close to being squashed in the parking lot after I left Bailey's?"

There was a pause, a long pause, while Carl floundered around for his least offensive words. He didn't flounder long enough. "Maybe the file was mislaid and the Bailey's incident was just an accident. It is a possibility, isn't it?"

No, it wasn't, because if it was, what did that make me? A paranoid who kept a messy desk. "Andrew Monogal has a knack for showing up at the opportune time."

"Andrew? Andrew saved Edward's life. He manages the mine, he is Peter's most valuable associate. They go back a very long time to their childhood in Austria."

Esterbrook and Monogal, the oldest of friends, the chairman and the CEO, the greyhound and the bulldog. "If Monogal manages the mine, I assume there is some sort of management contract between him and Peter."

"I'm sure there is, but I'm not that familiar with it."

"Why not? Lovell Cruse represents the Mother Lode, don't they? You're Peter's attorney."

"I do their legal work, but that particular contract was drawn up years ago, before I came aboard. I don't know all the terms."

"Didn't it ever occur to you that it might be a conflict of interest to be campaigning for the WIPP project when you represent the Mother Lode and your father-in-law owns it?"

Carl went into recorded message mode, candidate voice. "No, it didn't. I happen to think it will benefit an economically depressed area. Besides, polls have shown fifty-four percent of the voters in Bernalillo County are in favor of it."

"Spare me."

"As a matter of fact, Peter won't own the mine after today,

133

and I won't be representing it much longer, either," he said. "The agreement with the federal government will be executed tomorrow. It is important to get the documents signed quickly so there will be no question of conflict of interest in my campaign. The Department of Energy had some money available for acquisition, so now, whether WIPP goes through or not, the government owns the mine and Peter doesn't make any more money. The feds are confident that WIPP will pass, but if it doesn't, the mine will be leased and the land will be added to the national forest."

"And the national debt."

"Those are the facts, Neil."

"I don't suppose you'd like to hear the facts I found on my trip to Mexico."

"Peter owns the adoption agency, Los Niños de los Angeles. He said he told you that."

"He couldn't have told you himself somewhere along the way?"

Carl shrugged. I couldn't see him, but I knew he was doing it, shrugging. "That's the way Peter is. Maybe he should have told us, but he didn't, and I can't complain that he found us Edward."

Who could?

"Peter doesn't think I should let this incident intimidate me or make me back out of the campaign. We're not going to tell Celina about the notes, of course; she couldn't handle it. I wouldn't have gone to Peter without her knowing, but the way things turned out, maybe it's for the best that he and I are out in the open."

And just who did he have to thank for that? Me, Neil, a.k.a. Nellie.

"There's someone else out there who calls me Nellie. Did you know that?"

"So you said. But I don't think this is the time or place to discuss your lovers."

134

"It's not my lovers I'm talking about. It's someone who has been following me."

"Why would anyone do that? I'm afraid I must be going, Neil. It's a very busy day, and I have to be out of here by one. I'm putting in a campaign appearance in Bernalillo, and then I'm meeting Peter at the mine at six to work out some details of the contract."

"I'd like to suggest that you don't go there today. I don't think it would be wise, and I also don't believe that Kiefer is the solution to your problem."

"Neil, I hope you won't feel this is none of my business, but you've obviously been working much too hard. Maybe you should take some time off and go on a little vacation. Send me the bill for your fees and I will take care of it immediately, if that will help. By the way, I want you to know how very much we've appreciated your efforts."

And I wanted him to know how very little I appreciated his patronization. "Don't mention it," I snapped, and hung up.

I had other matters to occupy my time besides Carl Roberts. Judy Bates, for example. Suppose I got Ken to make the payments on the trailer and Judy to keep the dog with no visitation rights. Then Judy would recommend me to all her friends for their divorces and they would recommend me to their friends, a geometrical progression. On the basis of one contact with Judy I could spend a lifetime negotiating divorces. On the other hand, if Ken got extensive visitation rights and Judy had to pay for the kibble, he'd refer me to all his friend's wives. Either way, the highway would be littered with wrecked marriages. I didn't see any corporate mergers or patent infringement suits speeding by.

I wandered out to the front room, where Brink was hanging around talking to Anna, too busy to take on divorces.

"What's everybody doing for lunch?" I asked.

"We're going to Baja Tacos," said Anna. "Wanna come?"

Baja Tacos was a hole-in-the-wall with gut-wrenching

New Mexican food. "No, thanks. I don't feel like going out."

"We could bring something back if you want."

What did I want? A cold burrito with hot salsa? "How about a Grande Mac? Could you swing by there?"

"McDonald's?" asked Brink, raising his eyebrows, implying maybe that someone with my enlightened political views didn't eat at McDonald's. What was the difference, a lumpy burrito, a Big Mac? Cold meat was cold meat.

"I like to have a Big Mac now and then to stay in touch," I said.

I sat at Anna's desk while they were out just in case any new clients happened by. She had a bottle of Hold That Red nail polish in her desk and white-out in shades of white, buff, pale yellow, mint green, and pink. What she did with all those colors I didn't know; all I ever saw was the white that dropped like bird shit on my letters. I've heard that high school kids get high by sniffing the stuff. I opened the bottle, gave it a sniff, didn't like the smell, didn't get any higher. A woman in Texas invented white-out in her kitchen—I read that in *People* magazine. She mixed up a lot of batches on her kitchen stove before she got it right, but when she died she left forty million dollars.

After Anna and Brink got back I had my Big Mac, green chile, small fries, and large Coke with them just to be polite; then I went into my office and closed the door. There was a bunch of papers, records of phone calls, in an insurance folder on my desk. Carl had arranged them in chronological order: April 7th, May 8th, May 15th, June 3rd, and June 14th. He'd like to believe that May followed April, the 8th the 7th, *a* led to *b*, *b* to *c*, *c* to *d*. I rearranged them the way I remembered them: May 8th, May 15th, June 3rd, June 14th, April 7th. April 7th wasn't the first entry in Menendez's file, it was the last, and it wasn't four years ago either. April 7th, 2:30 P.M., twenty minutes, Señor Menendez to Esterbrook Farms. I flipped through my desk calendar. On April 7th I called Juárez and made an appointment with Menendez. On April

9th he was murdered. On April 13th Carl had his coming out party; on April 7th, when Peter Esterbrook was in Dallas buying the greater work of a lesser artist, Menendez-Jimenez called Esterbrook Farms and talked either to Lupe or to someone who watched the property when the master was away. The last entry on Menendez's desk calendar on April 9th had been *el perro dogo*, the bulldog, the dog who sunk his teeth in and wouldn't let go. What was it he wouldn't let go of?

The time had come to pierce the corporate veil.

I waited until I was sure Carl was clear of his office and then I called Angie. In Mexico you get by on bribery, here it's friendship. Sometimes it's easier to come up with the money. Angie had known me for a long time. It takes years to build up that kind of credibility, an instant to lose it. It was a rotten thing to lie to her, but I was willing to take the blame.

"Has Carl left already?" I asked.

"A half an hour ago."

"Damn. When I spoke to him earlier he said he would send Andrew Monogal's contract with the Mother Lode over by messenger before he left. I guess he forgot." It sounded like bullshit, even to me.

"You and Carl are working together again?" It was a question that hung on the wires.

"I'm looking out for Monogal on this one."

"That must be a treat. Just a minute, let me see if it's here."

"It's probably way in the back of the file; it was drawn up a number of years ago, before Carl joined the firm."

"That may take a little longer."

I listened to commercials while I waited: it was time to Stop & Shop.

"Well, here it is. You were right about the age of this thing; it's fifteen years old."

"Could you send it over by messenger?"

"I'd feel better if Carl were here; if he had mentioned it to me."

"I'm sure he just forgot, Angie. He's got a lot on his mind. If there's any question at all, I'll take the blame."

"Okay, Neil, if you say so. It's on the way."

A young man in biking shorts, black leather gloves, and headphones that didn't quite connect with his ears showed up shortly with the contract. It was an interesting document, fifteen years old, a profit sharing incentive plan and an option agreement. When the mine made a profit, Monogal received a percentage, and that percentage was applied toward an option to buy the place; he had fifteen years to come up with the full purchase price. It seemed generous enough: the manager was encouraged to manage and rewarded for his efforts eventually with ownership of the mine. It was drawn up at a time when nobody thought a remote gold mine in Lagrima would be worth much, when gold mining was pretty much a gentleman's hobby, interesting maybe on a portfolio, but not where the big ones were made. Of course, it would be impossible to estimate the value of anything fifteen years in advance, so the agreement said the price, to be determined at the time the option was exercised, would be "fair market value." In other words, whatever a ready and able buyer was willing to pay.

The fifteen years were just about up—they ended tomorrow, in fact—and Esterbrook had his buyer, the federal government, ready, willing and able to pay several million dollars more than Monogal could. It was a lot of money, but they had it, and they were getting a unique property, one whose geological formations supposedly made it suitable for storing nuclear waste forever. There weren't many areas like that around, and hardly any where the locals would welcome a nuclear dump for a neighbor. If they didn't like Peter's price, the government could probably have taken the property by the law of eminent domain and gotten it for less, but it would have been a lengthy process and this way they had that consummate politician, Carl Roberts, on their side.

138

The Mother Lode was the right place at the right time for the element of the nineteenth century (gold) to be replaced by the element of the twentieth (plutonium), and Andrew Monogal had just about lost control of it. This is what it all came down to, the basis of so many law practices: real estate and greed. It must have been option money already paid that Peter had so generously agreed to give back to Monogal yesterday in his study: it wasn't enough.

I picked up the phone and called the shop. "Could you do a job for me, Kid? It's a favor, but it's still a job. You'll get paid for it, and well, too."

"You don't have to pay me. I do you a favor anyway."

I explained what I wanted, but that he'd have to figure out how to do it. "You'll have to leave immediately," I said. Lagrima was two hundred twenty-five miles away, but the Kid could make it in three hours without even working up a sweat. "And when you get back be sure to report to me right away." I told him where to look if I wasn't home.

"Don't worry, I find you."

He didn't ask how much he'd get, although I knew he'd do it. But why? For love?

"For the adventure," he said.

Next I dialed the number of the Mother Lode office in town and asked for Monogal.

"May I tell him what the call is in reference to?" his secretary asked.

"He'll know," I replied.

Monogal came on the line. "Well, well. Ms. Hamel." He must have had one of those speaker phones that you can stand and yell at from across the room. It made him sound like he was speaking from the bottom of a tunnel. The echo effect emphasized the coarseness of his voice and an accent that he hadn't bothered to lose. "To what do I owe this pleasure?"

"I'd like to talk to you in person."

"How about this evening? This evening will be an excellent time to meet you, the best of all possible times. Be here at six. I am on Uptown."

"Where? In the Darth Vader building?" It was a recent addition to the Albuquerque skyline, a slab of black glass that reminded some people of Pueblo pottery.

He laughed. "Next door. The Mother Lode Building."

18

I DICTATED MY suspicions onto a tape and left the tape for Carl. I pushed papers around for a while and at five forty-five I put them back in their files. It was a fifteen-minute drive to the Mother Lode's office. In fifteen minutes I could have been out of the city, heading due west on I-40, out there where painted mesa meets celluloid sky, a quarter of an hour closer to Arizona. In fifteen minutes the Kid would be waiting near the gold mine and Carl would just be arriving. In fifteen minutes I could be right where I was now, .25 hours of billing time closer to Judy Bates's first divorce. In fifteen minutes I was in the lobby of the Mother Lode Building, pushing the button for nine, the top floor. Somebody had to.

The elevator opened directly onto the reception area and that room alone would have swallowed up Hamel and Harrison whole. The walls were paneled in dark wood with decorative moldings and a carpet of Sherwood Forest green. The receptionist's desk had a brass lamp with a green glass shade. The remaining light came from an office that opened onto the reception room, and through the open doorway I could see a wall-to-wall, floor-to-ceiling peach and lavender New Mexico sky.

"Good evening," Andrew Monogal said from the depths of that office.

He was sitting at his desk, silhouetted massive and jowly against the setting sun. It hurt looking into the sun, so I turned toward the wall, where I saw a map of the Mother Lode and next to it glass shelves full of ore samples, hunks of rock: red rock, black rock, brown rock, petroleum green rock; lined and flecked and mapped with gold. It was as if Monogal had ordered the sunset just to illuminate the gold.

"This is my favorite time of day. Be seated, please," he said, playing with a pencil stub, rolling it back and forth between his thick fingers.

It wasn't necessarily mine. I like to watch sunsets, but I don't like them looking at me. The New Mexico sun finds years you haven't even thought of yet. Every time the sun illuminated another vein of gold it etched another year on my face. The longer I sat on the other side of his desk, the older I felt. I lit a cigarette and added a few more years now, a few subtracted down the road. "Do you think you could close the drapes?" I asked.

"The sun will be gone in a minute, but for now take a look at the gold. You see, in the morning, when the sun is on the other side of the building, those rocks are just rocks. It takes insight to see the gold." His accent was just as unpleasant in person as it had been over the phone.

"You love the mine, don't you?" The sun slipped a little lower in the sky, climbed a little higher up the wall.

"It has been my life for forty years. Look at that." Just then the sun climbed to the top shelf and illuminated a dazzling hunk of ore.

He would lose all this—the grandiose office, the magnificent view, the alchemy in the afternoon. The sun climbed off the ore up to the ceiling and dropped behind West Mesa. He went from a gray silhouette to a gray human, surrounded by gold that had turned to stone.

"You and Peter Esterbrook go back a long time, I hear."

"A long, long time."

"To your childhood in Austria?"

"Yes. We were distant relatives, but I was the farm boy. Peter grew up in the village, more privileged than I even then. I became a Nazi. Does that surprise you?"

A man with his looks and charm? "No."

"Peter could have had a brilliant career in the Third Reich.

142

He was blond, handsome, well educated; he had the temperament for it. He probably would have become a general while I remained a soldier, but he saw the writing on the wall and he got out in time. Peter has a knack for getting out in time." Monogal was in a talkative mood, provoked by something. I wondered what: the twilight atmosphere, an attentive audience, a sense of accomplishment in a job well done? "Peter thought the Nazis were doomed to fail," he continued. "He saw the opportunities in America and he abandoned his country. I stayed, I served, I watched Austria die. When the war was over, I followed the path that he had made across South America and I tracked him down here. I was penniless; he was already successful, with a beautiful wife, a mine, an import-export business. I went to work for him at the mine. I worked there for him for almost forty years."

With a past like that, there probably wasn't much else he *could* do.

"But I don't suppose you came here to talk about my youth, did you?"

Maybe I had: the golden boy, the awkward friend; the greyhound and the bulldog; the runner, the latcher-on; the envied, the envious. Forty years in the shadow of Peter Esterbrook could ruin anybody's disposition.

"Has anyone ever told you that you, um, resemble a bulldog?" I said.

He smiled. That is, he rolled back his jowls and revealed teeth that were stubby and broken off, as if he had bitten down on something often and hard. "I have been called that on occasion. But we all have pet names, don't we, Ms. Hamel? Sometimes we like them, sometimes we don't. Now, just why *did* you come to see me?"

I didn't get to do it very often, but I still remembered how. In every cross-examination there is a time to parry, a time to jab. I went for it. "Because you killed Señor Menendez-Jimenez," I said.

He tipped the pencil up and began tapping the point against his desk. "Menendez-Jimenez, indeed. And what makes you think that?"

"You had the motive, you left the trail. On April seventh, when Peter was away, Menendez called Esterbrook Farms and talked to you."

"April seventh. Why would I remember that? Do you remember what *you* did on April seventh?" He smiled another stubby-toothed grin.

"As a matter of fact, I do. Menendez told you I was coming to see him and you had to find out why. On April ninth right before I went back to his office, he was killed. Your name was on his desk calendar, and you were the last person he saw."

"My name on his desk calendar? I don't believe that." Tap, tap, went the pencil stub.

"El perro dogo. That means the bulldog, in case you didn't know."

"Is that so? How very interesting. My Spanish, I will admit, is not very good, but I never saw the necessity to learn when there are people like yourself to interpret for me. You can hardly consider what you have told me as proof of anything."

Maybe, but he stabbed at the desk so hard just then that the pencil point snapped and broke off, as it had when he wrote the notes.

"You wrote those notes," I said. "When Menendez saw the note he connected it to you—something in your writing, maybe, your style—and he guessed what you were up to. That's why he asked me back that evening, to tell me. You killed him so he wouldn't reveal your sick scheme to me or to Peter."

"I didn't know you had such a strong imagination."

"And just what do you know about me?" It gets dark quickly in New Mexico once the sun has finished its dance. Shadows were already creeping into the room.

"Enough."

144

"More than enough. I've been followed, you broke into my apartment and stole the file from my office, and then you tried to run me down in Bailey's parking lot. The 'chick' doesn't much enjoy being pressed into the pavement, you know. The gold mine was your baby, wasn't it? And it was being stolen from you. You knew if Carl were scared out of running, the government would be in no hurry to negotiate with Peter. Carl's campaign was the leverage Peter had with the government, the cog in his machine. Carl is the only candidate in favor of WIPP. The government might be able to push the project through without him, but it would be a whole lot harder. With Carl in the race, Peter insisted that the deal be consummated now, because it would be unseemly for negotiations to drag on while Carl was campaigning, or, even worse, after he was in office. So Peter used Carl's campaign to get a bid from the Energy Department, a bid you'd never be able to match, making it impossible for you to exercise your option. I have a copy of that option, and I see that it expires at noon tomorrow."

"Where did you get that?" he snapped. The lights of Albuquerque began coming on one by one. People were going home, turning their TVs on, putting dinners in the microwave.

"I have connections. You worked very hard at that mine, didn't you? And it almost paid off. Who would have ever thought that 'fair market value' would turn out to be nine million dollars? Who would have thought there would even be another buyer? Peter probably found the only one in the world willing to pay big bucks for that place. You had fifteen years to come up with the money, and if you had only had the foresight and ability to do it before WIPP came along, you might be the one negotiating for nine million dollars. Your old buddy screwed you, and in return you left the door to Shep's pen unlatched, knowing he was Peter's most unreliable dog. You thought saving Eduardo would divert any suspicion from you and maybe scare Carl out of running and

145

that Peter would reward you with what you thought you deserved. He said he'd give the money you've already paid back, but it's not nearly enough, is it? Not when he's getting nine million dollars."

"Very inventive, Ms. Hamel. Any more suppositions?"

"Just one. I think you will try to prevent the mine from changing hands tomorrow."

"Most interesting of all. And how do you propose that I will do that?"

"I imagine in your long career you have learned something about explosives. But if you think you are going to damage anyone at the mine, if you think you are going to make Celina the heir and then convince her to turn it over to you, you are wrong. No one is going to set foot in there tonight. I've seen to that."

Monogal was a volcano that had lain dormant for too many years; he was about to erupt and spill hot lava all over whatever got in his way—the desk, the blotter, me.

"You bitch," he said. "You meddling fucking bitch! That man has everything, and what have I got after forty years? That mine belongs to me. I was the one who made it work. I offered Peter a reasonable price, I offered him everything I had, but it was not enough. He's selling it out from under me. However, you should be careful what you begin Ms. Hamel; you never know where it will end. You think you've got it all figured out, don't you?"

No, I didn't. There were too many pieces marked gold mine in this puzzle, too few marked Nellie, not one marked little boy. "Not everything," I said. "Why, for example, did your scheming revolve around Eduardo?"

He flicked a switch on his desk and a sharp, little light pushed the gathering shadows away and crowded them into the corners of the room. "Because Edward is Peter's son," he said. "Does that surprise you?"

The perfection of the father visited on the son. It didn't please me, but it didn't surprise me, either.

"The mother is Elena, a girl in Mexico, the most beautiful of all of Peter's girls. Being a Christian has never stopped Peter from liking girls. He talked her into giving up the boy. He told her Eduardo would have a better life in the States, but he didn't tell her that he was giving the boy to his own daughter."

"You've told her that?"

"Not yet. He is a very handsome boy, isn't he? A great joy to Peter. Peter had everything in life but a son, until Eduardo came along. Now he has everything."

I looked at the clock on Monogal's desk. Peter and Carl would be at the mine by now and the Kid would be waiting for them. It would be three hours before they got back.

"Maybe you've ruined my first plan, but I still have an option, you know." He was rolling the pencil stub again, back and forth across the desk.

No one would be at Esterbrook Farms with Eduardo but Celina, Emma, and Lupe. No one between Monogal and his "option" but me.

"You can't be considering that."

"No? And why not? It's very simple, I have what's his, he has what should be mine. He can turn the mine over to me, or I can take Eduardo back to Mexico to his mother. The choice is Peter's now." It was a twisted scheme, but what could you expect from someone who for one brief, shining moment thought the Third Reich was Camelot? "I'm not going to let you stop me, you know."

"There are people who know where I am: my partner, my friend. I left a tape for Carl."

"By the time he gets it ... "

That's why he had bared his jealous soul: I was there to listen, but I wouldn't be leaving to tell. He opened his desk drawer. Bulldog also happens to be the name of a pistol, and he had one of those, too—shiny, blue-black, snub-nosed and ugly.

The time had come to pull out *my* weapon, but all I car-

147

ried were my powers of persuasion, my quick tongue. "No," I said, "don't." It wasn't enough.

I pushed myself out of my chair in time to meet the pistol butt on its way down. The blow reverberated inside my head and sent me spinning into a starry void. The last thing I heard was a demented chuckle; the last thing I saw was his broken-toothed smile.

19

I WOKE UP in a hard, dark place tight as a shell, with no room to stand up, roll over, or even to pound on the wall and scream. Any part of me that didn't hurt was numb. It was tight and claustrophobic in there and I wanted out, except that it didn't sound too good on the outside either. At a distance at first, and then closer, I heard the shrill yapping of nervous and excited dogs. Caught between a hard place and a snarling dog, I sank into unconsciousness again. When I awoke my shell was bouncing and shaking, slamming me against the walls, sending ripples of pain through my head. It was moving, at a reckless clip, too, but at least it was taking me away from the dogs. I've always hated the sound of barking dogs; I hate it even more now.

The movement stopped. Then the shell jerked and popped open suddenly and I was exposed, a shucked clam, slimy and dull. A flashlight was shining in my face.

"Can you turn that thing away?" I said.

"Just wanna get a look at you. You don't look too good." It was a man's voice.

"So?" I said, "what do you expect?" I was trying to unbend a leg and stretch it, but it wouldn't move. It seemed like a nice place I had ended up in anyway, quiet, with fresh air, the smell maybe of piñons. I tried to take a deep breath, but it made my head hurt too much. "Who's there?" I asked.

"Me." He beamed the flashlight on his own face. It gave him a sort of devilish charm, lighting up his snaggly teeth, making shadows around his cheekbones and eyes. Sam. Who else?

"Oh, Christ," I said.

"Whatsa matter, Nellie? It could be a whole lot worse than me."

"I suppose so. It could be Monogal. What happened to him?"

"He's down the road at the big house. He had you loaded in the trunk of his car like a sack of chiles."

A big house, mean dogs, a very rich man. "Esterbrook Farms."

"You got it."

"I suppose you followed me there, too."

He grinned. "I saw you go into Monogal's office, I saw him come out. I was curious."

"You're gonna tell me why you've been following me, Sam. But first help me out of here." I suppose a clamshell would be a whole lot tighter without clam juice to keep it lubed, but that wasn't what made me feel so slick and cold.

"Shine that light on me again," I said.

"Now, Nellie, you'd be happier if you didn't see yourself. You're not lookin' so good right now." He turned the flashlight to the ground, lighting up the crowbar he'd used to get the trunk open, then flicked it off.

"Why am I so wet?" I didn't sound too good, either; my words were thick lumps that stuck to my tongue.

"You been bleedin.' It's just a face wound; they bleed a lot. But you'll be all right. Anybody who gets as mad as you do is gonna be all right."

"Just get me out of here." Sam reached under my arms and pulled me out. He stood me up, but my legs gave out and I stumbled and fell against him.

"I don't suppose you've got any tequila."

"I got a little whiskey." He leaned me against the side of the car, which, I happened to notice, was big and American, while he took the bottle from his pocket and poured some whiskey into my mouth. I could only open it a little bit to one side, and my lower lip hung loose. The whiskey dribbled down my chin. It wasn't doing me a lot of good there, but

150

some of it got through and set up a nice kind of glow.

"You have a rag or something I could clean myself up with?"

"Sure." He took his leather jacket off. Underneath it he was wearing a white T-shirt and he took that off, too. His chest was underbelly white, and his tattoos looked like bruises in the moonlight. Here in the land of enchantment where the heavens aren't so far away and the skies are always clear, there is sunshine and there is moonlight. From a sliver of a crescent to a hole in the sky, the moon shines in New Mexico. This night the moon happened to be full, the counterpart of the sun, only the light was softer, the shadows larger. The moon illuminated things daylight didn't.

Sam put his jacket back on, poured some whiskey on his shirt, and wiped at my face with it. "Don't worry, Nellie," he said, "I saw a lotta face wounds in Nam, and this one ain't too bad. They bleed a lot when they're close to the skin." Maybe, but I sure hated to see his shirt turning dark with my blood.

"Sam," I said. "You gotta tell me why you've been following me."

He grinned. "For the fun of it."

"You think this is fun?"

"Sure. Don't you?" He dabbed at my lip with his whiskey-soaked shirt. "I'll tell you why I followed you, but you got to tell me what you've been up to. Fair's fair. You willin' to do that?"

It was a matter of client confidentiality, but what difference could it make now? I'd tell him what I had to. "When did I meet you, anyway?" I asked, trying to remember. Was it a month ago? A week? Seemed like a lifetime—like more than one.

"We introduced ourselves that day on the highway, but I made your acquaintance long before that. You don't remember me, do you?"

"I don't remember much."

"You didn't know it, Nellie, but I was followin' you around the whole time you was chasin' that lawyer. Someone had plans for that guy, and they wanted to know what he was up to."

Was our secret safe from no one? "That's where you got the name Nellie from."

"That's it. I know a lot about you. I know what Carl called you, when he called you, where he called you, and why. But I didn't take no pictures or tape nothin'. I don't want you gettin' that idea. I only followed you as far as the door to the motels and your apartment. Why didn't you get that guy to spend some money on you? I always kind of enjoyed following you. You're a lively woman, too lively for him. I was sorry when you two broke up and I had to go back to drivin' a truck."

"I suppose Monogal was paying you for it."

"Sure, but Esterbrook was payin' him. They found me through Río Lindo, you know. I was ready to come back here. I needed a job, and following people seemed easy. What did I care who was payin' for it? I was gettin' paid, and not too bad either. Anyways, Menendez and me became friends when I was in Mexico, and it got so we was getting ready to put a few deals together: I knew the girls, he had the contacts. Esterbrook and Monogal may think they owned Menendez, but they didn't. We needed someone to represent us in Albuquerque, and I remembered you was a lawyer. I went to your office to see you that morning you got stuck on the highway, but you was already pulling outta your driveway when I got there. I had nothin' better to do, so I followed you. You made it easy by drivin' the same car. I never followed anybody who drove the same car half as long as you do. When your car broke down on the interstate that day, I stopped to help you out and say hello."

"Why didn't you tell me what you wanted then?"

"Because I wasn't s'posed to know who you was yet. When I went to your office I was gonna say I saw your sign out.

152

Anyways, when you made your appointment with Menendez, Menendez called me to see what I'd said to you, but I hadn't said nothin' yet, so Menendez got curious about you and called Esterbrook. But he got Monogal. Next thing I knew you went down there and Menendez was dead."

"Monogal killed him."

"I figured that, but I didn't have no proof, and I didn't know why for sure and you wouldn't tell me nothin' when I called you, or when I looked you up in El Presidente either."

"I couldn't, Sam. My relationship with a client is confidential. I'm only telling you now because the client and I badly need some answers."

"So who's the client?"

"Carl Roberts."

"Some client. I kept an eye on you, and when you went to see Leona I figured either you was lookin' for evidence or you was lookin' for a baby. Either way, we coulda helped each other."

"How'd you know I was going there, anyway?"

"Piece of cake. I watched you goin' into the travel agency and I asked the girl there where you was goin'. I told her I was sweet on you. She told me about San Miguel and that led to Río Lindo." He grinned, and checked my cut again. The bleeding seemed to have stopped, maybe the whiskey had sealed the wound. It made it feel better anyway. "You get anything outta him in there?" he asked.

"Nothing that could be used in court, but I know why he did it, and it wasn't because Menendez was doing 'business' with you. It's because Monogal worked for Peter Esterbrook for forty years thinking he was going to end up with a gold mine, and now Peter is selling the mine out from under him for a fortune. Monogal began sending threatening notes to Carl, thinking if he could scare him out of running for office, the government wouldn't be in such a hurry to negotiate with Peter and he would be able to exercise the option he had. I showed Menendez one of those notes and he figured it out.

Monogal's threatening to take Carl's adopted son back to his mother in Mexico unless Peter turns over the mine."

"That Monogal's a piece of work, ain't he?"

Since we were spilling confidences in the moonlight, there was one more question to ask him. "That wasn't your baby you were trying to sell in Juárez, I hope."

"He wasn't then, but he is now. Once Maria got hold of him she wouldn't let go. She's in Juárez right now trying to figure some way to get him out of there."

"What about the mother?"

"She don't want him. She's already got six."

Six, ten, one, two; these people playing musical babies made my head hurt even more.

"Whattaya wanna do now?" asked Sam.

"I want to go home, clean myself up, go to bed." I'd suffered a blow to the head, possibly a concussion, maybe even a fracture. The only thing that interested me more than my own bed right now was another shot of Sam's whiskey. "Give me another hit of that stuff," I said. "What'd you do with your truck?"

"Left it at Esterbrook's. I coasted into the driveway real quiet, put his car in neutral and rolled it away from the house. Then I hot-wired it and drove it here. I had a feelin' I'd find you inside."

"Monogal's probably in your truck by now with Eduardo, heading for the border."

"I got the keys, and he ain't got the skills to start it without 'em. He killed a man, Nellie, and you coulda been next. He didn't stuff you into his trunk because he was plannin' to take you to Rancho Encantado for the weekend."

That was true.

"What about the rest of the people in that house?" Sam went on. "That kid's not there alone. Monogal ain't gonna be in a good mood once he finds you and his car gone. He's got a mean temper. I seen it, Menendez seen it—you seen it too."

Who else was in the house? Emma, Lupe, Celina. There

is a saying here that if you save a man's life you become responsible for him forever. I have a saying, too: be careful who you harm.

20

WE HADN'T GONE far from Esterbrook Farms. It didn't take long to get back, not nearly long enough. We were met in the driveway by Peter's barking machines, the Dobermans, ugly mean creatures with pointed ears and tails, thin black bodies, narrow heads, and sharp white teeth. I suppose it was good breeding that made these dogs so tense and angry. Sam's truck was still there, just like he said it would be. The dogs closed in, gathering around the car and snarling viciously as we left the driveway, crossed the lawn, and pulled up at Peter's antique doorway.

"Why don't you shut the fuck up?" I said.

"You just stay down there, Nellie. Don't let him see you." I was curled up in the back seat, hidden behind Sam. It was the arrangement we'd made.

He turned on the bright lights and beamed them into the portal. We'd made our presence known; the next move was Monogal's. But he wasn't in any hurry to make it. The house was dark, with no sign that he or anybody else was there according to Sam.

"Maybe he's already split," I said.

"Not a chance," Sam replied.

"He must have someone he could call."

"If I hadn't cut the wires, he could."

"What was it you told me you went to jail for?"

"Car theft once, breaking and entering twice. I was good at it, too. I didn't get caught every time, you know."

"Good thing one of us has experience. Well, what are we going to do now?"

156

"Wait here."

But how long can you wait when a bunch of Dobermans want you for dinner? If this was a war of nerves, I'd run out of ammunition. "Why don't you just shoot those dogs?"

"Shh."

"What's happening?"

"He's put his hand out the door, motioning toward the ground. I'm gonna turn off the lights."

There was some whistle or command too subtle for us to hear, and the dogs shut up.

"It's about time," I said.

"I ain't lettin' you outta here till he calls those dogs inside." Sam rolled down the window and leaned out. "It's Sam. If you want your car back, call off the dogs."

I heard Monogal's voice then, dry leaves blowing in a cold wind. "They won't harm you. I gave them a command." I couldn't tell where the voice was coming from; the portal, the doorway. Wherever it was, it was much too close. I pressed myself a little farther into the upholstery.

"Inside," Sam called again.

Another inaudible command; I heard the front door shut. Sam handed me the truck keys. "Okay, Nellie, you got it? Give me about five."

"Be careful Sam. He's crazy, he's armed, and he's got the dogs."

"I got a gun, too, Nellie, but I bet I can take him without it. Guns give you the edge at a distance, all right, but up close I got somethin' even better." He tightened his karate-hardened right hand and chopped it against the top of the seat, making the car's radials quiver. He grinned at me, slammed the car door, and was gone.

Five minutes. How do you measure five minutes in the back seat of an automobile? I tried counting—one hundred, one hundred one, one hundred two—but I was too distracted. On the one hand they were five very long minutes, on the other they were much too short. I would have been happy to press my face into the upholstery and go to sleep. I would have been even happier to have this over with. When the moon had inched a little farther along the top of the seat, when it felt like Sam had been inside a lifetime, I opened the door, very quietly, checked to be sure the truck keys and flashlight were still in my pocket—they were—and looked around, just to make sure the dogs were nowhere to be seen. They weren't.

I let myself out of the car, leaving the door hanging open behind me; there's no sound that travels across the night like a slammed car door. Peter's lawn was silvery in the moonlight and I was alone on it, the only tree in his meadow, much too easy to see. I ran to the shadows near the house, which set my heart thumping and my head pounding again. When this was over I intended to find myself a stiff drink and a soft pillow. I inched along the side of the house, mashing down Peter's carefully tended flowers with apologies to Kiefer. It was Peter's fault, his arrogance that made this necessary. This close to the wall, I thought I might hear something from inside, a cry or a whisper or even a growl. But I heard nothing, nothing at all.

I got to the first corner, eased around it. Somewhere down this wall there was a patio, French doors. I saw the patio, and beyond it the silvery lawn and the dog pens, doors hanging open, empty. I made my way up to the door, which might or might not be locked. If it were, I could break one pane of glass and get in. Peter relied on his dogs for protection, that and his superior judgment of character, but who knew what effect the sound of shattering glass would have on this household, who would hear it, what the dogs would do. Sam was supposed to subdue Monogal and the dogs and keep Monogal in the living room, away from the den, but maybe he hadn't been successful. Monogal could be in the study waiting for me, a mass of broken stone behind Peter's desk. What did I have to protect me? A set of keys between my fingers; the Chi?

158

I reached the door, put my hand on the brass knob and turned it, pushed the door open. I was inside Peter's study, alone, standing on the Oriental rug. Not a sound within the house. It was not as silvery bright inside as it was out, but there was enough light to see by. I could see that there was no old Spot lying on the rug, that the bookcases were full of books, and that what I was looking for was hanging beside the door. It felt smooth as silver in my hand. The next step was to find out where everybody was.

There was something to be said for Peter's taste; the thick carpet, for example, moved me silently down the hallway. This seemed to be Peter's wing of the house. His taste was as predictable and imitative as Ralph Lauren's. His clothes closet was probably full of overpriced copies of L.L. Bean. Beyond the study I came to a bedroom. I flashed my light in and saw a huge bed smothered by a fur bedspread. It was immaculate, not a sock on the floor or an old pair of jeans or underwear thrown in the corner. Who lived like that? Men with Mexican maids. After that I found a guest room, twin beds, with neutral quilted spreads like in an expensive hotel room. A suitcase stood on a stand with filmy white things falling out. Celina and Carl's room when they were there. This wing was so quiet, it made me want to sing or scream, but I suppressed the urge. I looked out at the patio. The bougainvillea clung to the wall, the deer and goats watched it, the parrot slept in his cage, the fountain had been turned off.

I turned the corner into the children's wing. If there was anyone but Monogal and the dogs left in the house, it was a child. There was still no sound, not even a soft whisper in sleep. I reached Emma's room first. The door was shut. I stopped outside and listened; nothing. Either there was nobody in there or something I didn't want to see. As I couldn't linger outside thinking about that forever, I put my hand to the knob and pushed it open. The door slid silently across the carpet—even Emma's room was carpeted, I remembered: pale pink. Whoever was in that room made no

159

more noise than the Cabbage Patch Dolls, but when I flicked on the flashlight it lit up two pairs of eyes, red and frightened like the eyes of animals that you meet on the road at night. Celina and Emma were tied to the bed. The curtains had been ripped to shreds, the shreds had been used to tie their hands together, their feet to the bed, their mouths shut. Celina might have thought she was back in a nightmare again, finding me bruised and battered at the other end of the flashlight, but I guess it was an improvement over Monogal.

"It's Neil, Celina," I said.

"Um," was all she could manage.

The rags were cruelly tight, cutting into the skin around her mouth and hands, but otherwise she looked all right. Monogal had tied those knots, and there seemed to be bitter rage in each one. I managed to get Celina's hands undone first. "There isn't much time. The dogs are loose and Monogal has flipped out. Do you know where Eduardo is?"

She shook her head, and her eyes filled with tears.

"Don't cry now," I whispered. "You can do that later. I'm going to look for him. You get yourself untied and untie Emma so she can walk. It would be better if you left her gag on until we are out of here, as we have to be very quiet. Do you understand?"

She nodded and began to work at the knots. "You wait here. I'll be right back."

The next room was Eduardo's, still quiet, but as I approached I thought I could hear childlike breathing. The door was open. Eduardo lay in his bed, his teddy bear at his side. The eye in the center of the storm. Lupe watched me from her tiny chair as if she hadn't moved since I was last there, but she had put on a sweater, and a suitcase sat next to her on the floor, a sad south-of-the-border suitcase, held together with tape and hope, a suitcase that had carried a lifetime of belongings across the border and was getting

160

ready to take them back again. Lupe, it appeared, was cooperating with Monogal.

"Wake up Eduardo," I said. "We're leaving."

She looked at me without surprise, with a resignation that long preceded this event, that knew all about losing. Gringos were bigger, faster, better at business and motion.

"I'm awake," Eduardo said.

"Can he walk?"

"Sí."

"Up then. We have to hurry."

"He is taking him home, señorita," Lupe whispered, "to his mother."

Home, the place where children and flowers spring from dry riverbeds and dust. "Not really, Lupe. He's just using him to get what he wants."

"But he is not safe here, señorita. You saw what happen . . . the dog."

"That was Monogal's fault."

"I don't believe. He save Eduardo."

"There is more to Monogal than you think, Lupe. Believe me, Eduardo must go with Celina."

She stood up then and helped me lead the boy into the next room, where Celina had untied Emma, mouth and all. "Who is that lady, Mommy?" she said when she saw us. Celina began to cry. "Oh, Edward, my baby," she said, "my baby." Time was not on my side. Somewhere in this house were two men, one crazy, one questionable, and a pack of vicious dogs.

"Okay, everybody," I said, "let's go. *Andale.*" I shushed them and marched them down the hallway. Celina carried Eduardo, whispering to him all the way. I hurried an unwilling Emma along. It wasn't going perfectly, but more smoothly than I might have hoped. Too smoothly. We were close to the den when Emma spoke up. "I don't want to go," she said—loud.

161

"Shh," I replied. I bent over to pick her up, and in that instant Lupe grabbed her suitcase and stepped into the shadowy courtyard. She slipped past the leather chairs, the bougainvillea, the terra-cotta pots, into the corridor that led to the kitchen, and, beyond that, the night and another country. Shadow in shadow, she was gone. Eduardo watched her go, and I had the feeling he could see her a whole lot longer than I could.

"Where is Lupe going?" cried Celina.

"I don't want to leave," Emma said sulkily.

"Oh yes you do." I gave her a good smack on the fanny and she responded enthusiastically.

Her efforts didn't go unnoticed. There was the sound of a strangled cry from the living room.

"Here," I said to Celina, "these are the keys to the truck that is in the driveway. Go through the den and get the children out of here. Go to Carl's office. The Sikh guard there will take care of you. Tell him to send someone to help, quick."

"Neil," said Celina, "how can I ever thank you?"

"Please. Just go."

This was one part of the plan Sam and I hadn't worked out: was I to stay or to go too? Someone—Sam—had saved my life, someone was responsible, and I found myself in the Prado room once again. Sam had Monogal under control just as he had said he would, with no sign that he had had to use a gun. Monogal's own gun lay across the room on the floor, as if he had drawn it and Sam had chopped it away. Jungle-fighter skills had triumphed over superior weaponry once again. Monogal hadn't been let down gently, however. He sat furious and deflated in one of Peter's stiff red chairs. "Look," Sam said when he saw me. "Your sack of chiles. She's not looking too bad, is she, from spending the night in your trunk."

I don't suppose I looked great in a bloodstained shirt, my

eyes turning black and blue, but Monogal blanched as if I were a zombie returned from the dead—which apparently was the fate he'd planned for me, to be dumped off somewhere along the interstate, a meal for the coyotes and the crows, one of those piles of teeth and bones that turns up around the time that everyone has forgotten about you.

"So sorry to disappoint," I said.

Outside the window, beyond the red velvet drapes, we heard a door slam, an engine start, hesitate, stall. "You're letting them get away," screamed Monogal, lunging forward, his face screwing up in rage.

"Yup." Sam pushed him back.

"Cool it, Sam," I said.

"Hey, Nellie, this is the guy who carried you all the way down the freight elevator and dumped you in his trunk. Is that any way to treat a lady?"

The truck coughed again, hesitated, then caught, spinning gravel as it took off down the driveway. "No," cried Monogal, listing like a limp balloon.

"Don't go limp on me, man," Sam said. "That's no fun."

"Where are the dogs, Sam?"

"Your friend here shut them in the kitchen so we could have a little talk. Didn't you, big boy?"

Monogal didn't reply, slumping a little farther down in his chair.

"You killed Menendez," said Sam.

"What do you care?"

"He was my partner, my friend." He gave Monogal a playful little slap that left a red welt on his face. A touch of malice beneath the fun.

"What do you want? Money?"

"Nope."

"Knock it off, Sam."

"You knock it off, Nellie. I been wantin' for a long time to get my hands on this guy."

163

Monogal pursed his lips and made a blowing motion, but no sound came out, or maybe it was a sound that was too high-pitched for me to hear.

"This guy's pathetic, ain't he? He keeps doin' that, thinking his dogs will come. But they're locked up in the kitchen, ain't they? I helped you do it."

"Sam, wait a minute—Lupe went out through the kitchen."

"Lupe? Who's that?"

"The Mexican maid, Sam. Remember?"

There was a high-spirited, gleeful yelp, the sound of scrambling claws.

"You fucker." Sam grabbed Monogal.

Monogal smiled his shitty, stub-toothed, little-boy grin.

In about two seconds the dogs filled the doorway, black bodies leaping through the air, white fangs flashing, barking in happy chorus. "Here, boys," Monogal called. "Him." Sam could have used a gun now, but they pounced on him before he had time to go for it, grabbing his pants leg, pulling him down.

"Get off me," he yelled, flailing at them.

A dog turned in my direction, pushing me back against the wall, waiting for a final command before moving in for the kill. I wasn't relishing the prospect of having my face ripped open by a bunch of Dobermans, and I put my hand up to protect it. The other hand pushed deep into my pocket.

"Good boy, Vronsky," said Monogal.

The dog crouched. If dogs could laugh, he was. I had one opportunity, and it was in my pocket, smooth as silver. "Now, Vronsky," commanded Monogal. Vronsky went for me with a joyful snarl, fangs bared in a grin. This was the moment he'd waited his entire life for. No trainer's padded arm was at the end of that leap, just me, my own tasty flesh and blood. My hand closed around the whistle. I brought it to my lips and blew it in Vronsky's narrow face. He fell back and looked at me with disappointment and confusion in his black eyes.

"Now!" screamed Monogal.

But the dogs stopped snarling and hesitated just long enough for Sam to leap up, jump on Monogal, and put his fist in his mouth, just long enough for Sam to grab Monogal's arm, twist it behind him and yank. I heard the bone pop. I saw Monogal's face turn white and tears fill his eyes. I saw his options fall away like leaves in November.

"No, boys," he cried. "Hold it. Not now."

21

No ONE IN that household ever saw Lupe again. She disappeared into the night, or into Mexico, which is similar enough. Sometimes that country seems like a dream, brilliant, confused, full of flowers and birds, demons and flies. Andrew Monogal was carted off for psychiatric evaluation and probably extradition to Mexico for the murder of Menendez-Jimenez. As I had suspected, he'd also blown up the Mother Lode, hoping that Carl and Peter would be part of the explosion, but the Kid kept them out of the way.

Carl and Peter were willing to forget about the mine for the pleasure of seeing Monogal knit sweaters in a Mexican jail and the benefit of not having the publicity of a trial. No charges were filed for the kidnapping attempt or the attack on me. When Carl and Peter asked me if I wanted to pursue the matter they made it clear that the publicity would be a disaster for all concerned. Except me, of course. How would it hurt me? But I agreed. It made life simpler for them, but that wasn't why I agreed. Monogal was a broken man, not one of whose dreams had come true, unlike Peter Esterbrook, most of whose dreams had. But if you measure a man by the quality of his dreams, what did that say? Peter was forced to level with Carl about Eduardo, and they agreed that no one else was to know the truth of his parentage. That meant not Celina and Eduardo, not me, I already knew. But it was a client confidence, privileged information. I didn't intend ever to tell. I hoped no one would ask.

Carl came by one day to pay my fee, and he brought the child with him, which was a nice gesture. Eduardo's little shirt hid most of the damage. A scab on his neck might leave a scar, but it wasn't terribly noticeable. His eyes had changed, though; they had gotten bigger and darker and about a hundred years old. Carl told me that Eduardo never mentioned Lupe, that he never even asked about her, but Celina was terribly hurt by Lupe's desertion and for a while that was all she could talk about.

"Maybe that's all she can afford to talk about," I said. Monogal was written off as a man who had cracked, Lupe had been unduly influenced, Sam's and my presence explained by the coincidence of our having been doing work for Monogal when he cracked. It wasn't a story that bore a lot of thought. "You can't really blame Lupe," I said. "She believed that Eduardo was in danger."

Carl shrugged. "Did she have to let the dogs out of the kitchen?"

"I'd like to think that was an accident. She had to go through the kitchen to get out of the house. She was distraught. She probably didn't think to lock the door and the dogs just pushed it open."

"Well, we'll never know for sure, will we?"

Carl had left Eduardo in the waiting room with Anna while we walked. She thought he was the cutest *precioso* she had ever seen. If Mexican children turned out this beautiful, she was probably wondering if she shouldn't start looking for a Mexican to father hers instead of George, the blond computer salesman. But when you get right down to it, most people are happier with children that look like them. It's easier to confront another culture in one burst of sensuality or anger than to face it calmly every day. Even Peter Esterbrook had made the decision to look on from a distance and let someone else actually raise his child. Carl's famous adaptability was working on his behalf. He was capable of putting the fact that Peter was Eduardo's real father out of his mind for the most part, and recent events had, if anything, made him and the boy closer.

Carl sat down and laid the bill that Anna had prepared on my desk. He took out his pen and thing-of-beauty checks, but before he started to write, he said, "If you need more, just say so."

"I laughed. I knew where every penny of that check was going: the back rent, the payments on the copier, the telephone bill. What would we do with the extra money, anyway? Buy Anna a word processor?

"Just pay the bill."

"I can't tell you how much we appreciate what you've done, Neil, all of us."

"Please," I said.

"It's the truth, whether you want to hear it or not."

"I don't."

Carl looked good, like the bottle had been recapped with the fizz back in. Ready now, I could see, for the race, and with that kind of enthusiasm he'd probably win.

"Will the explosion change WIPP's negotiations for the mine?" I asked him.

"No. It's the geological formations and the land they are interested in, and that's still there—maybe rearranged a little. The agreement has been signed."

So the WIPP project would most likely go through, the trucks would thunder across Lagrima with their lethal loads; uranium and plutonium would lie among the gold.

"The explosion was unbelievable, Neil. It knocked us off our feet and we hadn't even entered the mine yet. We would have been right in the middle of it if that young man hadn't blocked the bridge across the arroyo with his truck and kept us from driving up the road. When he refused to move his truck, Peter insisted we'd go up anyway—we'd walk. So thanks to him, we were still a half a mile away when the place blew. By the way, don't we owe him something, too?"

"He's covered in my bill."

"Is he a, um, friend of yours?"

168

"My mechanic," I said.

"Monogal and Peter go back a long time. Who would have thought that losing the mine would make him crazy?"

"Anybody but you and Peter."

Carl let that one go by and handed me the check. "Well, I guess that covers it. Peter made a settlement with that guy, Sam. He's kind of sleazy, don't you think?"

"It was your father-in-law who hired him to follow us in the first place."

"I know, Neil. I'm sorry. I don't approve of everything Peter does; you know that. But I have to live with him."

"Sam saved my life and kept Eduardo out of Monogal's hands." Why was I defending Sam? Why not?

"You're right," said Carl. He closed the checkbook and put it in his pocket. "Oh, by the way, Peter offered Kiefer his job back."

"Did he take it?"

"No. He said he'd live on berries and bugs before he'd ever work for Peter again."

"I guess being a good judge of character isn't always enough."

"Everybody makes mistakes, Neil."

"But not everybody thinks they're perfect."

Carl stood up. "Well, I guess our business is through."

"It is, except that I hope Angie will forgive me for lying to her."

"I explained that it was necessary and she understands. Well . . . thanks again."

"It's nothing."

I walked him to the door. Anna had Eduardo at her desk, coloring in a coloring book that she kept around for slow times. "I hate to let this little guy go." She wasn't the first to have that feeling.

Carl picked Eduardo up and the boy leaned over his shoulder and waved as they went out the door. "Bye, Neil," he said.

"Bye, sweetheart," I replied.

I had the Kid over for dinner and made my specialty of blue corn tortillas, Monterey Jack cheese, and salsa, which I call Chile Willies. You break the tortillas into chip-size pieces, sauté them until crisp, drain them, then heat them with the salsa. When the salsa is hot, you put thinly sliced Monterey Jack on top, cover it and simmer until the cheese is melted. I serve it with pinto beans. The Kid loved it. He ate every bit and asked for more. He could eat like that at every meal and stay thin as an aspen. For dessert I served vanilla Swiss almond and chocolate fudge ice cream together.

"I park my truck across the bridge and wait," he told me. "I was worried the rattlesnakes would be out, but I see nothing, only rocks and shadows and then these guys come in different cars. They look like father and son."

"Close."

"I tell them you say not to go up the road but to wait. They don't like it, but I won't move my truck and they have to walk. Before they get there, *kaboom!* one big explosion lights up the whole sky." He shook his head. "How you know there would be an explosion?"

"I didn't. It was just a hunch."

"You want to go to the racetrack with me next time you have a hunch?" he said.

"Don't blow this there." I had a check for him. I had charged a hundred and twenty-five dollars an hour for his time, Carl's rate. Why should the Kid work for less? Although it was a lot more per hour than he got for fixing cars or playing the accordion.

"This much?"

"You deserve it."

"You tell me, chiquita, if you ever want me to work for you again."

"Don't worry," I said.